Unmasked AT MIDNIGHT

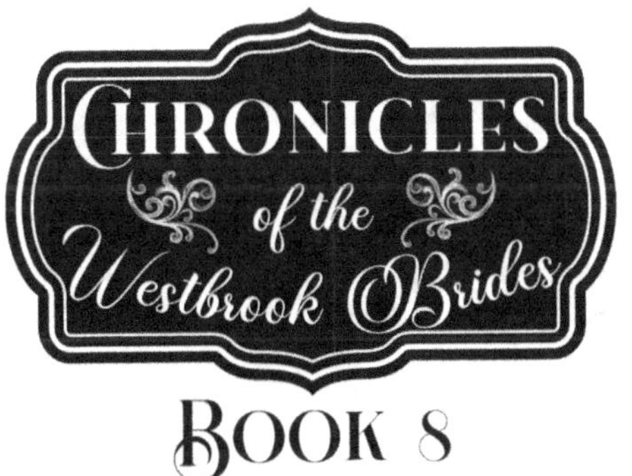

BOOK 8

Blue Rose Romance® LLC

"You dance well,"
Darius murmured
into her ear...

His warm breath caused
a shudder to ripple from
Araminta's waist
to her nape.

USA Today Bestselling Author
Sweet to Spicy Timeless Romance
COLLETTE
collettecameron.com
CAMERON
Blue Rose Romance LLC

PRAISE FOR...
COLLETTE CAMERON®

See What Readers Are Saying About
Collette Cameron®

★★★★★ "...a fast and delightful read with plenty of heart and humor."

— BOOKWORM 2 BOOKWORM

★★★★★ "Collette Cameron has an amazing skill with historical romances."

— NIGHT OWL REVIEWS

★★★★★ "Cameron conveys the tone of the Regency era well... highlights for the reader how far we've come as women in society..."

— RABID READERS REVIEWS

UNMASKED AT MIDNIGHT

A ROMANTIC OPPOSITES ATTRACT MYSTERY & SUSPENSE FAMILY SAGA REGENCY ROMANCE

CHRONICLES OF THE WESTBROOK BRIDES
BOOK EIGHT

COLLETTE CAMERON®

GET YOUR FREE BOOK!
THE REGENCY ROSE®

JOIN MY EXCLUSIVE MAILING LIST
AND GET A FREE EBOOK!

Plus Sneak Peeks, Giveaways, Contests,
Exclusive Content and More...
P.S. I promise only good stuff ~ no spammy stuff!

Scan the following QR Code to join
The Regency Rose VIP Group Mailing List
and get your FREE BOOK!

Thank you,
Collette Cameron®

THE
REGENCY
ROSE®
VIP
CLUB

ACKNOWLEDGMENTS

Thank you to Rachel Ann Smith for inviting me
to participate in the
Lords and Ladies of St. James series,
where UNMASKED AT MIDNIGHT
was first published.
Your organizational skills astound me!

For my first grandchild.
I love you, precious little one, even though
God took you to Heaven before we met.
Your Gigi

ONE

Woodhaven, Cumberland, England

APRIL 1828 ~ MID-MORNING

There she is—the woman I mean to court.

Lord Darius Westbrook took in Eudora Clarke's loveliness. Her beauty—silky brunette hair, creamy ivory skin, an oval face, rosebud pink lips, and a petite but superbly rounded figure—filled him with awe, even from across the street.

Peeking from beneath a feathered bonnet, her soft doe-like eyes framed by lush sable lashes, Eudora gave Darius a demure smile. Her mother, Mrs. Gertrude Clarke, narrowed her sharp gaze on him, her features hardening into severe lines in her rather mannish face as she said something to her daughter.

It confounded him how a woman as plain and unremarkable as a sheet of foolscap and with a figure resembling a lumpy cotton bale could have produced such a beauty. Only the Good Lord knew the answer to that mystery. Still, as dour and unapproachable as Mrs. Clarke was, no one could fault her diligence in chaperoning her only offspring.

Eudora dutifully averted her gaze, but not before her smile widened a fraction in rebellious flirtation.

To Darius's utter delight, the delectable Miss Clarke wasn't quite as biddable as she appeared and as, no doubt, her formidable mother preferred.

He wasn't the least deterred by Mrs. Clarke's disapproval.

A prize easily won was no prize at all. The pursuit, overcoming obstacles, and emerging victorious made the quest all that much more worthwhile. Darius would win over Mrs. Clarke and court Eudora.

Of that, he had no doubt.

Enough woolgathering. Back to work.

He studied the sign he'd just hung outside his establishment with a critical eye before touching one side ever-so-slightly to bring the slat into perfect balance. His twin, Cassius, had painted the beveled rectangle, flawlessly capturing the establishment's welcoming atmosphere.

A musical giggle drew Darius's attention to the delightful feminine bundle swathed in lavender and pink across the cobbled village square.

Eudora was the essence of womanliness.

And yet, a question continued to niggle in his mind; would his mother and sister like her?

An octagon fountain burbled happily in the spring sunshine as a pair of round-cheeked urchins—amid squeals of delight—floated their sailboats in the makeshift sea. Men lifted their hats and dipped their chins as Eudora and her imposing mother meandered along, stopping to peruse the window displays.

Glowing, Eudora glided from shop to shop.

Mrs. Clarke glowered and lumbered in her daughter's wake.

Darius waited for the ping of jealousy his rivals' attention should warrant, but nothing so unpleasant disturbed the morning's serenity. Likely because of his confidence that Eudora returned his regard. Surely she must. Else, why would she seek his company despite her mother's censure?

A year ago, the mere thought of courting a woman would've sent him hightailing it to the farthest corners of the earth. But then, a year ago, he'd still held a commission in His Majesty's Navy and wasn't the proud owner of Westbrook's Book & Coffee Emporium, his bookstore and coffeehouse.

Excitement and anxiousness battled for dominance when he thought of the week-long grand opening in just two months.

He'd invited several authors for the event, including his brother Leonidas. His mother had suggested the authors come masked on the final evening to add intrigue and to see if the guests could guess who they were. Mother, who had planned too many grand events to count, insisted the finale include refreshments and a string quartet. Darius didn't mind the former, but the latter seemed more conducive to a Society ball.

Nevertheless, he conceded to her recommendations.

After all, the duchess was a force to be reckoned with and her organizational expertise was legendary.

Invitations to the more prestigious guests had gone out weeks ago, while a sign in the window invited the locals to participate in the daily activities as well. Naturally, the Westbrook brood, including Grandmama, and his parents, the Duke and Duchess of Latham, would be in attendance.

Westbrook's Book & Coffee Emporium welcomed everyone, especially the vivacious and breathtakingly lovely Eudora Clarke. Although of marriageable age, Eudora exuded a girlish charm. Her bubbly temperament and winsome smile had captivated him from the first day he'd met her at Saint Andrew's Church.

So immersed in his thoughts about Eudora, Darius

tottered unsteadily when the sturdy ladder he stood upon teetered.

What the...?

Jostled from his romantic musings, he glanced down, unsurprised to see his twin grinning up at him.

He countered his brother's grin with a glower.

"You're gaping at her like a moonstruck swain, Dare."

Cassius didn't appear the least contrite for almost toppling Darius off the ladder.

Ignoring his brother's teasing, Darius descended a couple of rungs and, with great satisfaction, examined the store's bay window. The display needed a few more books and other reading-related doodads before he would consider it completed, but it was coming along quite nicely.

Satisfaction burgeoned behind his breastbone. Compelled by grit and determination, *he* had done this, not his father's wealth and influence.

His twin continued to grin like a drunken buffoon.

"I'm grateful you delivered the sign in person, but shouldn't you return to your art studio in Brighton, Cass?"

"No." Cassius shook his head. "No, I don't believe I shall."

Darius tamped down a surge of annoyance. "I'm sure you have eager patrons vying to have their portraits painted."

There was a time Darius worried his twin would never paint again.

"My patrons can wait. Besides, you know I always bring my supplies with me. I might even dabble at a landscape or two while I'm here." Cassius leaned a shoulder against the doorframe. Deep blue eyes, so like Darius's, glinted with suppressed worry as he rubbed his chin. "In truth, I determined just this morning that as a good brother, I ought to remain and lend a hand. Perhaps I'll stay for a few weeks. I might even recruit Layton to assist."

Bollocks.

Betrayal and cynicism had skewed their half-brother Layton's view on marriage and on life in general. The taciturn eldest Westbrook sibling was the last person Darius wanted advice from.

"*Lend a hand*?" Darius released a snort worthy of a Royal Ascot racehorse. "Spying on my courtship of Miss Clarke, you mean."

"Guilty." Cassius burst into laughter. "It's my duty as your twin. We've already had multiple siblings charge headlong to the altar with undue haste. I'm here to assure you don't make the same mistake. Did you forget our vow of bachelorhood?"

A young man's immature declaration.

Cassius had been scorned in love, as had Layton. Naturally, neither brother had an interest in marriage.

"Courting her is not a proposal, Cass," Darius said

dryly. He might very well find they weren't as compatible as he hoped. If he fell in love, he wouldn't mind a quick union either.

Besides, was it truly a mistake to marry for love, even if Society deemed the wooing rushed? Despite their relatively short courtships and improbable matches, his siblings, Leonidas, Althelia, Adolphus, Lucius, and Fletcher, were all ridiculously happy.

Darius supposed he would have to wait and see how his courting progressed. Easier done without an interfering twin hanging about or a brooding older brother who had as much use for marriage as he did carbuncles.

Darius had chosen Woodhaven as the location for his establishment as much because of the quaint but growing township's charm as the proximity to his father's ducal estate—a mere forty-five-minute carriage ride away.

Convenient, but perhaps too much so.

In the past week alone, Mother and Father had come unannounced thrice to check on the bookstore's progress.

Or, more aptly, to see if their second youngest child's foray into the world of commerce required financial assistance—which it did not. Despite his rather meager naval compensation, Darius had saved enough capital to invest in the venture, thanks to adhering to a frugal budget, along with investments from his writer-brother Leonidas and his half-brother Fletcher, who owned two successful social clubs.

The only ripple was how Darius would support a wife—
if he decided to propose—in the manner she was accustomed to until the bookstore became solvent. He didn't mind economizing—it taught a person discipline and prudence, and also built character. However, as certain as he was that red blood pumped through his veins, he was equally convinced that Eudora would not appreciate frugality.

Taking a deep breath of the refreshing sea air, he shoved that disconcerting truth to a corner of his mind to examine later.

Love conquers all.

Was he in love with the fetching miss?

Something very pleasant burbled behind his ribs and warmed his blood. Surely that was love or something very near the emotion.

Darius Ethan Trent Westbrook, you are in suds up to your starched neckcloth.

Yes. Yes. I am.

And he couldn't summon a jot of concern about his newfound infatuation.

As if sensing Darius's ruminations, Mrs. Clarke glanced over her sturdy shoulder. Her squarish features granite hard, she gave him a scorching *you-better-not-behaving-impure-thoughts-about-my-daughter* glare.

Rather than give her a cocky salute and an unrepentant grin, as had been his first instinct, he dipped his chin deferentially. No point in adding fodder to the blaze he wanted to extinguish.

"The dragon is breathing fire today, I see." Echoing Darius's thoughts, his twin veered his gaze toward the Clarkes.

An unapologetic social climber, Mrs. Clarke was a fearsome foe. Darius had determined that truth from their very first meeting and the ensuing stilted conversations. Eudora, on the other hand, didn't seem as concerned with social standing as her mother.

Despite his father's title and his family's powerful influence in Society, as a younger son, Darius was clearly low on the matron's list of appropriate suitors. Nevertheless, he suspected, Eudora typically got exactly what she wanted.

Darius just needed to ensure she picked him.

Her mother would most likely come around.

After all, didn't all parents desire their children's happiness above all else?

His parents always had.

A horrific thought invaded his mind, bringing his romantic musings to a grinding halt.

Would Eudora expect her mother to live with them?

Ye gods.

No force on earth would compel Darius to share a domicile with that she-dragon. He expelled a deep breath.

He'd have to cross that bridge when he came to it. And right now, that bridge was some distance away.

"She's just a protective mother," Darius said, hoping to convince himself. "With a daughter so lovely, she has to be."

"If you say so." Cassius's tone conveyed he didn't believe that to be the case. "I think she just doesn't like you. You're not inheriting a peerage, nor are you wealthy."

"Thank you for pointing out those deficiencies, brother," Darius drawled, his tone dryer than hearth ash. Though, in truth, Darius didn't consider his lack of a peerage title a detriment, nor was he a bloody pauper.

"I know you are infatuated, Darius, and I shall not besmirch Miss Clarke's character, but she's not the sweet, biddable miss she pretends." Genuine concern and affection softened his twin's features. "I've already discerned that from the short time I've been here. You are blind to her faults. Trust me when I tell you my ears are burning from the tales I've been told. I fear you are dashing headlong into a tempest."

"You would have me listen to gossip too?" Darius snorted, betrayal rooting around his belly. "You could at least pretend to like her for my sake."

Cassius shrugged. "I shan't dish out platitudes to soothe your ego."

"When have you ever?" Darius snapped.

"Exactly so, and that is how you prefer it. And not

that you need reminding because I know how intelligent you are, but the truth is still the truth, even if you refuse to believe it." His expression somber, Cassius disappeared inside the bookstore.

Why did the rotter have to be right?

Head bowed, Darius sighed.

Was he running headlong into a storm?

Having several older brothers in line for the duchy ahead of him might have much to do with Mrs. Clarke's disapproval. Or mayhap it was that Darius had determined to pursue his passion and open a bookstore and coffeehouse and therefore would smell of the shop.

Eudora's tinkling laugh drew his attention. She shook her head at something her mother had said, causing her parasol's pink fringe to jiggle. A seaborne breeze had the temerity to tease a glossy curl near her cheek, and Darius heaved another deep sigh.

Yes, he could be quite content in Woodhaven.

But would it be with her?

He took another step down the ladder.

A series of outraged, muffled *honks* interrupted his admittedly moon-eyed regard of the delectable Miss Clarke.

Hunched over and wearing a gown in an indeterminable shade of brown—or was it drab-green?—a slender young woman bore down upon him. Her rapt attention remained riveted on a fat goose waddling ahead of her.

"Sir Waddlesby!" she huffed, grabbing for him and missing. "You are in so much trouble."

Sir... Waddlesby?

Oh, she meant the goose.

An embroidered cobalt blue band encircled the goose's neck, and he clasped a cherry-red glove firmly in his beak.

Darius had no idea that geese could run so fast.

The gander's speed was impressive.

Honk-honk. Honk-honk.

Passersby stopped, laughed, and pointed as the woman chased the naughty wing-flapping fowl.

"Sir Waddlesby. Stop this instant. That is not your glove," she panted as she pelted along, the goose remaining just out of her reach. "It's Mrs. Tenney's, and if you ruin it..."

Just as Darius stepped onto the last rung, Sir Waddlesby spied the ladder and dove between its wooden legs.

If a goose could grin in triumph, that dratted creature did.

The recalcitrant goose's pursuer realized too late what her ill-mannered pet had done. She tried to stop but barreled full-on into the ladder. In a tangle of limbs, ladder rungs, and feathers, Darius landed atop the woman with a resounding thud.

TWO

Outside Westbrook's Book & Coffee Emporium

TEN AWKWARD SECONDS LATER

"*Oomph.*"

"Oh!"

Honk. Honk.

Bystanders guffawed and tittered, plainly enjoying the unfortunate display.

Cassius rushed from the bookstore, stopped short, and emitted a sound that was something between a snort and a cough.

Darius could well imagine the tableau of him lying sprawled atop the young woman whose face he couldn't quite make out, given that the pesky goose had now inserted itself between them, nuzzling their heads and flapping his wings.

Cassius cocked an eyebrow and, with mirth twitching his lips, lifted the broken ladder and set it aside. "I'm afraid to ask."

"Then don't," Darius growled, pushing the goose away, now seemingly intent on making amends for his unchivalrous behavior. The elegant glove which had caused the commotion lay abandoned on the pavement.

"*Ahem.*"

Darius glanced downward into round, shockingly green eyes framed by golden-tipped lashes. Several tendrils of her straw-colored hair had escaped her chignon, and the riotous curls poked from her head like miniature springs. She smelled of sunshine and grass and spring flowers.

"Would you please remove yourself from my person?" the unnamed woman asked, her voice slightly breathy.

And why shouldn't she sound breathless with his six-foot frame pressing her flat as a Scottish oatcake?

Her goose gave an affronted honk and nipped Darius's shoulder.

Twice.

"Ouch. Stop that." He tried to swat at the winged gallant, but the deuced gander scooted aside before diving in again, pecking Darius on the backside, and then swiftly retreated with a goosey cackle.

Devil take it.

Was the feathered menace laughing at him?

The crowd certainly was.

Cassius hooted in hilarity. "Oh, this is rich."

"He's trying to protect me," the young woman explained, despite her obvious embarrassment, as she dragged a hand from between their bodies to gesture toward the maddening creature. "Sir Waddlesby thinks he's a dog and likes to play fetch with gloves."

Shaking his head, Cassius chuckled as he bent and retrieved the glove in question, adorned with exquisite embroidery. "It's a lovely glove."

"*Harrumph.*"

Darius's attention riveted on a pair of very shiny, very large shoes before he gravitated his focus upward.

Ah, hell—

He bit back an ungentlemanly oath.

Mouth as tight as a hen's hind end, Mrs. Clarke glared at him, disapproval fairly radiating off her stiff form. She turned a censorious gaze onto the woman he still half lay upon.

Standing beside her mother, her forehead creased in a puzzled frown beneath her pink bonnet, Eudora wavered her attention between Darius and his feminine assailant.

"Lord Darius? Aren't you going to get off her?" Eudora asked, her dark eyes wide and guileless, though the merest shadow of annoyance or irritation lurked in their depths.

Darius shoved to his feet with admirable alacrity, considering his stinging posterior and bruised ego, before plowing a hand through his hair to restore order to the strands poking every which way. A feather floated off his shoulder, and another tickled his cheek. He swiped the offending reminder of the fowlish assault away.

Cheeks apple red, the young woman gracefully shifted to a sitting position, yanking her ugly brown gown over her shapely calves. A gray and white feather floated onto her lap. Another stuck out from the remains of her chignon, most of her lovely hair having tumbled around her shoulders in a cloud of springy, flaxen curls.

Her goose wasted no time waddling onto her lap and draping his neck across hers. At once, she wrapped her slender arms around him.

All was forgiven, it seemed.

Despite the awkwardness of the moment, Darius found their interaction touching. He'd never known anyone with a pet goose, but he couldn't deny their genuine affection for one another.

"*That* goose is a menace, Miss Weldon." Mrs. Clarke gave a disdainful sniff and lifted her chin. "He ought to have been consigned to the cooking pot years ago. You'd be wise to serve him on a platter for Christmas dinner."

HONK! Hiss. Hiss.

Sir Waddlesby bobbed his gray and white head menacingly toward the outraged matron, who had the good sense to retreat several paces.

"Goodness, Araminta." Eudora wrinkled her dainty nose. "I imagine it must mortify you to make such a spectacle of yourself." She touched her smooth, neatly coiffed locks. "My word, your hair..."

Darius furrowed his forehead.

Surely genuine concern prompted Eudora despite her comment having the air of a veiled insult.

"Yes, quite," Miss Weldon agreed with the bravado of someone accustomed to humiliating scrapes—likely caused by Sir Waddlesby. She combed her fingers through her unruly curls in a vain attempt to tame the wayward tresses. Upon coming in contact with the wayward feather, she plucked it from her hair with a chagrined grimace.

Sympathy stirred behind his ribs.

No one enjoyed being on the receiving end of laughter and ridicule.

The young woman set her goose down. "Stay there. You've caused enough ruckus for one day."

Sir Waddlesby bowed his neck, apparently penitent. Or perchance, the shiny black pebble by his foot had caught his attention.

Peck. Peck.

"Allow me." Cassius extended his hand to assist Miss Weldon.

Once on her feet, he handed her the glove. "I hope the glove is salvageable."

"Thank you." A wistful smile tipped Miss Weldon's rosebud mouth upward at the corners while she carefully folded the satin, then tucked it into her pocket.

Her keen-eyed goose watched until the crimson cloth disappeared.

The feathered fiend released a long breath and made a humming noise.

Could a goose sigh in disappointment?

A stab of irritation toward his brother for being so quick to assist the young woman and for being the recipient of her winsome smile speared Darius.

Brushing off her gown, Miss Weldon faced him, her expression solemn. "I beg your pardon, my lord, for toppling your ladder. I didn't see you."

Mrs. Clarke made a rude noise—somewhere between a grunt and a jeer. "*That* is as obvious as your reconstituted gown, which you no doubt sewed yourself."

Darius scowled at the woman's calculated cruelty.

Mrs. Clarke was a nasty piece of work.

"Mama!" A giggle escaped Eudora before she clapped a gloved hand over her mouth.

Nervousness at her mother's blatant rudeness or laughing at Miss Weldon's expense?

One was understandable. The other was wholly unacceptable. And Eudora's youth was not an excuse. Even a child knew the difference between compassion and unkindness.

Was this what Cassius had hinted at earlier?

Was Eudora's cheerful disposition a façade?

Self-castigation speared Darius. Was he on the verge of falling in love with a woman because of her physical attributes without knowing her character?

That made him a shallow bacon-brain.

"You must be the bane of poor Reverend Weldon's existence," Mrs. Clarke said, continuing her tirade. "He really ought to exhibit more control over you."

Reverend Weldon?

Of Saint Andrew's?

Why hadn't Darius noticed Miss Weldon during Sunday services?

Miss Weldon didn't respond, but a fresh wave of color sluiced up her porcelain cheeks.

"Excuse me." Cassius leveled the Clarkes with a dark glance before slipping away.

Darius realized he hadn't responded to Miss Weldon's apology, and though she held her head up, there was no mistaking the chagrin shadowing her vibrant eyes.

"It's of no consequence, Miss Weldon." Except for his bruised pride and another black mark against his character by Mrs. Clarke.

Chest heaving in indignation, Mrs. Clarke clomped away, calling, "Come, Eudora."

"Good day, Lord Darius." Eudora gave him a flirtatious smile. "I look forward to attending your store's grand opening."

"Eudora!" her mother snapped.

Eudora dutifully followed her mother, but not before Darius observed a mutinous glint in her brown eyes.

Instead of collecting her goose, Miss Weldon eyed the inside of the bookshop longingly.

"What a delight to learn we'll have our very own bookseller in Woodhaven. I adore books. I operate a small lending library out of the parish salon. 'Tisn't much, but there's such a need." She waved a delicate hand toward the market square. "Woodhaven has long needed a bookshop. Might I ask if you intend to carry novels by Ann Radcliff? Rosa Matilda? Madam Quillheart?"

So, Miss Weldon was a romantic, was she?

Darius toed aside a broken ladder rung. "I plan on providing an assortment of books to appeal to various tastes. I've also invited several authors to give readings at the grand opening."

"You have?" She tapped her tulip of a chin. "Invited authors for the grand opening? Oh, how marvelous."

"Indeed." He nodded. "I'm not familiar with the last author you mentioned. I presume the name is a nom de plume?"

"*Hmm?*" Miss Weldon cast Darius a distracted glance. "Oh, yes. Madam Quillheart."

She cleared her throat.

"At least, I think so. But her books are splendid. Very daring and modern, but also with engaging plots and fascinating characters. So are Jane Austen's. Though she wrote anonymously as By a Lady, her authorship was an open secret."

Her focus veered toward the open shop door. "Do you mind if I take a gander inside?"

Gander?

Was the pun intended?

Somehow, Darius thought it very much was.

Miss Weldon possessed a sharp wit.

"Well, actually…" He didn't want the public moseying about inside his establishment just yet.

Without so much as a by your leave, Miss Weldon scooped up her obnoxious goose and entered the bookshop.

THREE

Inside Westbrook's Book & Coffee Emporium

A FEW SECONDS LATER

Araminta had to escape inside. Her humiliating tumble would be the talk of Woodhaven. Papa might even insist she get rid of Sir Waddlesby or—God forbid—*cook* him, as Mrs. Clarke had so rudely propounded.

No. No.

Araminta could not even begin to contemplate such a horror.

How could she eat her pet?

Granted, he *had* been intended for Christmas supper when Mr. Delbert had gifted the reverend the gosling

25

three years ago. Naturally, the care of the young gander had fallen to Araminta. Since her mother's death five years ago, Araminta had overseen the parish and household duties, except for Papa's weekly sermons, of course.

She couldn't help falling in love with the gander, who did quite behave like a cheeky puppy. Araminta adored Sir Waddlesby, and he was a most loyal and loving pet, even if he tended to get into mishaps on an almost daily basis.

The begging and pleading she'd undertaken to convince Papa not to eat Sir Waddlesby had been most persuasive. Thankfully, her father had finally conceded to her wishes. The family had enjoyed a rather skinny chicken that Christmas instead.

Inside the bookstore, Araminta inhaled deeply, relishing the aroma of beeswax, leather, new books, and coffee.

Sir Waddlesby hummed against her chest—his way of expressing contentment.

He wasn't an utter nuisance.

He ate slugs and kept stray cats away from the garden beds; no better watchdog could she ask for. Nevertheless, the goose's obsession with gloves had caused more than one fracas. After this latest fiasco, if Papa didn't insist on exiling Sir Waddlesby, he would most likely demand confining the goose to a pen.

Holding him close, Araminta shuddered at the notion.

Humming to herself, she glanced over her shoulder and caught sight of Darius Westbrook entering his establishment. She swiftly pretended absorption in the thoughtfully organized and cheerful interior.

A glossy counter and a coal stove dominated one side of the L-shaped main room. The light from the windows streamed onto angled rows of bookshelves, some partially lined with crisp new books. Several comfortable chairs and sofas, arranged in cozy sections, invited readers to explore the books at their leisure.

Though not ready for customers yet, the bookshop was taking shape.

Araminta's half-boots clicked on the parquet floor as she ventured farther inside. Still humming, she continued her exploration.

Sir Waddlesby hummed in contentment too.

They made a ridiculous duo, but she didn't give a flying fig.

The entire back area of the bookstore remained vacant still.

How wonderful and most opportune.

A perfect place to tuck a small lending library.

A peek into the largest adjacent room revealed the coffeehouse section of the establishment. Sleek square walnut tables and chairs filled the room's center, and several alcoves contained additional overstuffed chairs, side tables, and small sofas.

A staircase at the far side led to an upper floor.

No doubt the living quarters, which, given the size of the main floor, were quite extensive.

Obviously, a great deal of thought and planning had gone into the bookstore and coffeehouse's design. Though unfinished, the tastefully decorated establishment exuded a welcome and charming air.

What a marvelous addition to Woodhaven.

Araminta tried not to think about her rather embarrassing introduction to Lord Darius Westbrook.

How was she to know Sir Waddlesby would careen into Lord Darius's ladder?

It wasn't the first time her dear goose had gotten her into a scrape, and it certainly wouldn't be the last. She heaved a deep sigh and kissed the top of Sir Waddlesby's head.

What's done is done.

Besides, she was far more interested in Lord Darius's delightful bookshop than in reliving her earlier mortification.

At least, she thought she'd crashed into the twin who owned the bookshop. Then again, she couldn't be positive. Unlike her twin sisters, Laurella and Callidora, the Westbrook brothers resembled one another so greatly it was difficult to tell them apart.

Her much younger sisters were as different as night and day. Laurella possessed Papa's chestnut hair and brown eyes, while Callidora had Mama's blonde hair and green eyes, as did Araminta.

Araminta had planned on calling at Lord Darius's establishment prior to the grand opening and requesting permission to use a shelf or two as a lending library. She also hoped to ensure Lord Darius carried Madam Quillheart's books.

Not only did Quillheart garner fame for writing novels featuring scandalously romantic stories, but her books also continued to gain popularity—which secretly brought joy and pride to Araminta, who, in fact, was Madam Quillheart.

Araminta bit back a smile as she patted Sir Waddlesby's silky feathers. No one, not even dearest Papa or her sisters, knew that she was a published author who wrote under the Quillheart nom de plume.

Papa would have an apoplexy if he ever found out. As the rector of Saint Andrew's, her father considered himself the moral compass of Woodhaven.

The shame. The sin.

His daughter writing such scandalous twaddle.

Lord above.

However, that scandalous twaddle generated a tidy income, thank you very much.

Papa still believed the sale of her embroidery work provided the occasional joint of ham for dinner, the

Cheshire cheese he liked so much, the fine port he indulged in, and the *London Weekly Times*.

Lord knew the funds didn't come from the so-called *generous* offerings collected every Sunday.

Araminta almost scoffed aloud but settled for the slightest skewing of her upper lip.

How absurd that several of the community's loftiest members, who perched so regally upon their pews every week, adorned in their Sunday finest, regularly pointed out others' supposed sins while presenting themselves as the most virtuous of congregants. They were, by far, the stingiest people who held tightest to their purse strings.

Mrs. Clarke's dour visage sprang to mind.

A proverbial miserly hypocrite if ever there was one.

The only thing Mrs. Clarke ever offered was unsolicited advice and constant condemnation.

Papa would be even more shocked if he knew Mama had encouraged Araminta's writing.

Looking back, Araminta understood that her beloved mother must've known for quite some time that she was not long for this world. She never quite recovered from Laurella's and Callidora's births and had passed from this world when the twins were but five-years-old. At nineteen, Araminta had become a surrogate mother to her sisters.

Nevertheless, Jane Weldon had done everything within her limited means to help ensure their family had financial security by imparting her talent for embroidery to Araminta and, more importantly, by encouraging her daughter to submit her books for publication. Mama had even helped Araminta choose Madam Quillheart as her nom de plume.

The giggles they'd shared coming up with the pen name.

Stinging tears misted Araminta's eyes, but she blinked them away.

"Miss Weldon, I haven't opened to the public yet," Lord Darius said from behind her.

"Please forgive my intrusiveness, my lord."

An opportunity had fallen into her lap, and she couldn't waste it.

Swiftly blinking away the moisture pooling in her eyes, she shifted the hefty goose to her other hip. Pasting a bright smile on her face, she turned to face the handsome bookshop owner.

"You are Lord Darius Westbrook, the proprietor?"

"I am." He began unpacking books from a wooden box and setting them on a nearby shelf.

Araminta couldn't help but notice how his shirt-sleeves and silver and black jacquard waistcoat stretched over his taut muscles as he moved.

Of course, she already knew who *he* was.

His tall form, dark hair, and navy blue eyes had drawn her attention at church since the first day he'd attended.

Araminta also accepted he had *no* idea who she was.

She wasn't feeling sorry for herself. It was the truth. Tall, slender, fair, and without a single new gown to her name, she couldn't compare or compete with Miss Eudora Clarke's sable-haired loveliness.

The pampered and spoiled beauty's lushly rounded figure and lavishly styled gowns had gained her another admirer—just like many other smitten, eligible bachelors in the area. What a shame that men were such shallow creatures and didn't realize Eudora's charms were only skin deep.

Still, it wasn't for Araminta to inform Lord Darius of Eudora's shortcomings.

How could she do so without sounding petty and jealous?

Never mind that she'd been on the receiving end of Eudora's unkindness for years and had first-hand knowledge of the soul-deep meanness that fetching smile concealed.

Lord Darius lifted a full crate of books onto another crate, and Araminta found herself mesmerized once again, this time by the bulging muscles in his forearms.

Get on with it.

She cleared her throat.

"I promise I shall leave you to your work directly, but I have a proposition for you." At least her gumption hadn't completely deserted her despite the embarrassing fiasco that initiated their meeting.

He cocked a raven eyebrow in askance. "Oh? And what might that be?"

Araminta couldn't blame him for his reticence. She hadn't exactly been at her best when she knocked him from the ladder in front of half the township, including Eudora and Mrs. Clarke.

Eudora couldn't quite conceal her gloating at Araminta's humiliating mishap, but Lord Darius hadn't seemed to notice. Or maybe he had and didn't care.

That thought didn't sit well in her belly.

If only Araminta could relive the last half hour.

The day had begun innocently enough. She'd put bread on to rise and spent an hour in the garden. Her shabby work gown smudged with dirt, she had just entered the parish kitchen to put the bread on to bake. Arms full of firewood, she'd left the door agape, and Sir Waddlesby had seized the opportunity.

He'd snatched Mrs. Tenney's newly finished glove off the table and tore off like the hounds of hell chased him. Araminta had spent a fortnight embroidering the gloves, and Mrs. Tenney was supposed to take delivery of them tomorrow.

Naturally, Araminta had no choice but to chase her errant goose through town.

"Yes, Miss Weldon. I confess. You have stirred my curiosity as well." Lord Darius's equally handsome twin brother sauntered over and leaned a shoulder against the same bookshelf Lord Darius stacked books on.

Araminta examined the brothers, studying every element of their countenances. *Hmm.* She tapped her chin with her index finger, contemplating their identical features. And yet... "Ah. Yes. Now I see the difference."

The brothers exchanged flabbergasted glances.

"You do?" the unnamed Westbrook twin asked. "We used to switch places when we were boys, and not even our parents could tell."

Lord Darius's skeptical glance spoke for him.

He didn't believe her.

Well, Araminta would prove it then.

She gave a firm nod. "I do."

Shifting Sir Waddlesby once more, Araminta wagged her finger at Lord Darius. "You have more pronounced grooves around your mouth, Lord Darius."

She angled her finger toward the other twin.

"While you have deeper creases across your forehead, my lord." Cocking her head, she smiled. "I would venture that Lord Darius is the more precocious, jolly, and daring twin, while you, my lord, are the more serious, sensitive, and practical."

Lord Darius's brother's jaw dropped.

"By God, Dare, she pegged us. Spot on."

Araminta shrugged, then tilted her head. "I have

younger twin sisters. One is more gregarious and the other more demure. A common occurrence, I dare say."

The laugh lines bracketing Lord Darius's firm mouth and the slight furrows creasing his twin's forehead provided a convenient way to tell them apart. Her attention lingered on Lord Darius's mouth for a moment—lips just the right fullness.

Not too thick or thin and not moist and slobbery. Unlike Clarence Button who always had wet lips and was forever trying to steal a kiss from her.

Araminta couldn't prevent the shudder that rippled across her shoulders at the recollection of Clarence and his grasping hands.

"Might I ask what your name is, sir?" She spoke to the as-yet-unnamed twin.

How very forward of her. Still, the men had been rather lax about introductions.

The twin bent into a courtier's bow as Lord Darius returned to placing books on the shelf.

"Lord Cassius Westbrook, at your service."

"Yes, of course. Your father is the Duke of Latham." Heavens, her arms ached. Sir Waddlesby needed to go on a reducing diet. "That makes addressing you easy, then. Lord Cassius and Lord Darius, I am Araminta Weldon, the eldest daughter of Reverend Zebedee Weldon."

"What is this proposal you mentioned, Miss Weldon?"

Lord Cassius asked, giving his brother a rather gloating glance.

She sucked in a bracing breath. "I propose a quiet corner in the bookshop to operate a lending library. Many people in Woodhaven and the surrounding area cannot afford to buy books, yet love them just the same. I could bring my library here and occasionally purchase new volumes to lend to patrons."

Only rarely.

Funds remained tight even when she received her quarterly royalties.

"A grand idea." Cassius clapped his hands. "What say you, Darius?"

Lord Darius had turned to study her. His intense scrutiny in the bright room made her nervous. Even if he said no, she wouldn't quit trying. Everyone deserved a chance to read, not just those who could afford to purchase books.

"I think...the idea...has merit." Speaking slowly, he shifted his attention to his twin.

A grin splitting his handsome face, Lord Cassius nodded. "I'd wager Mother and Father have several volumes at Hefferwickshire House that they would be happy to donate."

"Really?" Such a wave of relief engulfed Araminta that she almost dropped Sir Waddlesby. He released an indignant honk, and she set him on the floor. After withdrawing a length of string from her other pocket, she tied it to his collar.

"I am so grateful, my lords. When may I call upon you to discuss the details?"

"Tomorrow. Come for tea," Lord Cassius answered before his brother had a chance to. "No sense wasting time. We'll need to organize a suitable area for you before the grand opening."

"Indeed." No enthusiasm riddled Lord Darius's droll response. "Can you bring a list of your current collection? We'll need to discuss your hours of operation and how you will prevent patrons from walking out with books that are for sale."

"Of course." Giving an eager dip of her chin, Araminta angled toward the door. She must get home. She'd been gone far too long as it was. The rising bread likely had spilled over the bowl by now. Papa and the twins would want luncheon. "What time shall I call tomorrow?"

It had been so easy.

Lord Darius was a good sort—not at all what she'd expected from a duke's son.

She had been prepared to present her case, beg, cajole, and plead on behalf of those who loved reading and books but had little money to afford them.

"Four o'clock." Lord Darius picked up another stack of books. "Oh, and Miss Weldon?"

She turned back. "Yes?"

"Leave your goose at home." He gave Sir Waddlesby a pointed look. "I don't want goose excrement on my new floors."

"Oh, he's trained. He only goes outside."

Doubt drew his lordship's firm mouth downward.

"Nevertheless, this is an establishment for humans— not glove-stealing, impertinent geese." Lord Darius hadn't forgiven Sir Waddlesby's bad manners, it seemed.

As if sensing he was being discussed in unflattering terms, Sir Waddlesby raised his head and let out a displeased honk.

"Of course, my lord," Araminta quickly agreed. "He'll remain at home."

Hopefully.

Once outside, she couldn't prevent her triumphant smile. It quickly faded as Lord Darius's harshly uttered words carried out the open door to her.

"Why did you do that, Cassius? Of all the bloody hairbrained ideas. I have enough to do to prepare for the grand opening. Now you've saddled me with a provincial chit's idealistic dreams for bettering mankind."

Disappointment sluiced Araminta, stealing her previous joy.

Lord Darius toppled off the pedestal she'd placed him on.

She'd not make that mistake again.

FOUR

Westbrook's Book & Coffee Emporium

THE NEXT DAY ~ FIVE MINUTES TO FOUR

Darius glanced at the bookstore entrance as he made his way to the coffee room, where a table had been set for tea.

No sign of the impudent Miss Weldon yet.

A lending library *was a* good idea.

But was establishing it in his new bookstore ideal?

Already seated, Cassius hooked an ankle over his knee as he helped himself to a Shrewsbury tart.

"You could've said no, Dare."

A thread of censure deepened Cassius's voice. Of

course, he knew what Darius was thinking. It had always been thus with them.

"You don't believe a lending library benefits the community?" Cassius asked.

"Of course I do." His left knee cocked, Darius rested one hand on his hip and the other on the back of a chair. "I'm simply unsure this is the right time or location. How will we prevent customers from waltzing out of the bookshop with new volumes?"

"*Ahem.*"

As fetching as spring sunshine in a sky-blue gown and a straw bonnet with a matching blue ribbon tied beneath her chin, Miss Weldon stood just inside the coffeehouse entrance. A rather bedraggled and worn leather satchel hung from one slender shoulder.

"I can answer that question, Lord Darius."

How had Darius not noticed her before? For the undeniable truth was that Miss Weldon was imminently noticeable. In fact, she was quite unforgettable, with or without her deuced goose.

He searched near her feet.

Thank God.

No bloody goose today.

Cassius sprang to his feet. "Do join us, Miss Weldon."

"Thank you." She beamed at Cassius.

Darius's twin tossed him a gloating glance.

Cassius was welcome to the chit. Lovely though she

might be, Miss Araminta Weldon was also impudent, brash, and had an odd notion of what constituted a pet.

Besides, Darius had his eyes on another prize with molasses-dark hair and eyes.

Except, now that he'd met Miss Weldon and had taken to heart what Cassius had observed about Eudora, he no longer felt as convinced as he had yesterday about pursuing Eudora. At least not with the intensity he had before.

There was no need to rush things.

He would use his head and not his heart. Or was it merely his libido that had turned him into a beef-wit of late?

"Yes. Do." Regardless, Cassius's gallantry made Darius appear a churlish sod. "I would like to hear your solution, Miss Weldon."

After settling gracefully onto the chair, Miss Weldon slipped the satchel strap from her shoulder and withdrew a pair of well-used ledgers from their leather enclosure. She flipped the top book's cover open, and Darius couldn't help but notice her mended gloves were void of the beautiful embroidery adorning the one her pet goose had stolen yesterday and that had led to their calamitous meeting.

After resuming his seat, Cassius snatched another tart.

Darius slid into a chair as well.

"Each book from the lending library shall be clearly marked inside the cover," she said.

Darius hadn't noticed the lyrical huskiness of her voice yesterday. Probably because he'd been distracted by his very public tumble, Mrs. Clarke's seething disapproval, and Miss Weldon's wholly unexpected proposal.

A small rectangular bookplate affixed to the inside cover read *Woodhaven Lending Library, Established 1828.*

She'd made the simple template herself, but Darius could not fault her system for identifying the library books.

Miss Weldon tapped the page. "Each book is numbered as well, and I created a system to catalog authors and titles, keep track of borrowers, and when the book is due back."

"Impressive, Miss Weldon," Cassius said with an approving smile.

Indeed, it was. This project meant a great deal to her, and for reasons Darius did not understand, he was reluctant to destroy her dream—even if it might inconvenience him.

He lifted the teapot. "Tea, or would you prefer coffee?"

Her extraordinary green eyes rounded.

"I've never tried coffee. May I?" She gave a delicate sniff. "It smells divine."

"Of course." Darius poured three cups of coffee. He

slid the cup and saucer toward her. "The flavor is quite bold by itself. I suggest you add milk and sugar."

She peeled off her gloves and, after laying them aside, took a delicate sip.

Darius couldn't help but notice the many red needle pricks dotting her fingertips.

"I see what you mean." She added a generous portion of milk and three sugar lumps. After stirring thoroughly, she ventured another sip.

"That's delicious." A pleased smile arched her pretty mouth. "Robust yet smooth."

Cassius glanced at his pocket watch.

"Regretfully, I have an engagement. A potential portrait client." He rose and straightened his coat. "I hope you can convince my brother to permit you a portion of the bookshop. No one should be deprived of the joy of reading."

"I quite agree, my lord." Miss Weldon offered Cassius a pretty smile.

His brother bowed and took his leave.

Nothing like tossing Darius under the carriage.

Not only would Miss Weldon consider him an ogre for denying her request, but his denial wouldn't endear him to the locals. He could not afford to alienate the townspeople, a fact she had likely counted on.

He couldn't decide if he applauded her cunning or if her cleverness made him leery.

Thanks to the insidious seeds of doubt Cassius had successfully planted yesterday, Darius now mistrusted Miss Weldon and Eudora. Except Miss Weldon's motivation was entirely anthropic and not self-serving. In truth, setting up the library would create even more work for the already overburdened vicar's daughter.

Darius had asked around that morning—subtly, of course. And not only had he learned a couple of unsettling tidbits about Eudora but also several things about Miss Weldon.

Since her mother's death five years ago, Miss Weldon had been tasked with being her father's hostess, housekeeper, mother and governess to her two younger sisters. She accepted commissions for her exemplary embroidery work. Not to mention chasing an ill-behaved, glove-stealing goose all over town.

How did she propose to find the time to run a lending library too?

Nonetheless, Darius had promised her the opportunity to persuade him, and he was a man of his word.

"Shall we continue discussing your proposal, Miss Weldon?" Darius selected a ginger biscuit and then lifted the plate. "Would you care for one?"

"No, thank you." Taking another sip of coffee, she closed her eyes. "*Mmm*, that is so good."

A rush of profound desire flooded his senses at her innocent and unknowingly provocative response.

He crossed his legs lest his physical response become apparent.

What the devil was wrong with him?

He was interested in Eudora.

Yes, but that was before I met Araminta.

STOP.

Darius had a complicated enough life. By thunder, he would not muddle it further by acting like a fickle debutante who couldn't decide which beau she preferred.

Miss Weldon pointed to her list, the angry red pinpricks on her fingertips a stark contrast to the pale paper. "In addition to all the library books being labeled and kept in a separate, clearly marked section of the bookstore, the library would only operate during specific hours while I am here. I would suggest a prominently displayed sign clearly stating the library's hours."

"Go on," he urged, enjoying the sound of her husky voice. It soothed him in an unexpected and inexplicable manner.

"We could cover the shelves and rope or block off the library section outside lending hours." She paused, and a small furrow creased her forehead. "I am forgetting something."

Her expression cleared, and her green eyes sparkled.

Green always had been his favorite color.

"Oh, my father says I may come on Mondays, Wednesdays, and Thursdays from one to four in the afternoon. He thinks a library and bookshop can only benefit the community."

Darius nodded. At least he wouldn't have to deal with the lending portion.

That was a relief.

His budget didn't permit additional hired help just yet —only Philip Sherman to prepare the food and operate the coffeehouse. In time, Darius hoped to hire a cook and servers for the coffeehouse and clerks for the bookstore too.

"What if someone wants to return a book when you aren't here?" He blew on his coffee before venturing a taste. Strong and black. Just how he preferred it.

"I can leave a crate marked *Book Return* behind the counter or just outside the library's roped-off area." She fished in the satchel for a minute, then withdrew a few sheets of foolscap. "I made a list of the books I currently loan out."

Her eyes glittered with excitement.

This venture was important to her. He found her enthusiasm touching.

"I've operated the library out of the parish salon for over three years."

She'd subdued her riot of flaxen curls into a chignon, though he doubted she'd ever achieve the sleek perfection of Eudora's glossy tresses. Oddly, he'd thought of Eudora much less since yesterday. Miss Weldon, on the other hand, had consumed his thoughts.

Well, not *her*, but her proposed library, of course.

"How old are you?" he blurted

Her mouth went slack, and her eyes widened. "I beg your pardon?"

The query surprised him as much as it did her.

He scrambled for a reason to have asked the rude question. "You possess a rare maturity for a young woman."

She arched a winged eyebrow. "Are you calling me old?"

"No." He fervently shook his head.

Miss Weldon laughed, and Darius's heart flipped over.

How could it be that in a day, she'd wriggled her way into his life so much that he had allowed her a lending library in his bookstore, that he was reevaluating his interest in Eudora Clarke, and he had experienced a more potent reactions to Araminta than any woman he'd ever met?

"I'm teasing you, my lord." Humor twinkled in her eyes and creased the corners of her mouth. "I am four and twenty."

Not that much older than Eudora but far more mature.

To distract himself from her tempting mouth, Darius pulled the paper toward him and quickly perused the three pages written in tidy script. There were approximately two hundred books. It was not a vast library by any means, but given how expensive books were, it was an admirable collection.

No doubt his parents could add another hundred at least, and perhaps he and his family could spread the word that they sought books for a lending library.

Darius tapped his fingertips on the table.

From the beginning, his goal had always been to make the emporium a welcoming place for everyone from lord to lad, pauper to prince, doctor to debutante, and widow to waif. He hadn't considered why anyone who could not afford to buy a book or a cup of coffee would venture inside.

A lending library provided the missing element.

They could open the library for the next two months until the emporium's grand opening. He would know by then if her endeavor was worth continuing. "Let's say I agree to your proposal for a probationary period. If I decide it isn't working, I expect you to remove your books without complaint."

Leaning back, Darius scrutinized Miss Weldon.

"Understood, but I think you will find the arrangement most beneficial. Even though a patron might consider the cost of a book too dear, they still might want to purchase a cup of coffee, tea, or a bookmark."

She'd read his mind.

"Then we agree." He extended his hand, and after a moment, Miss Weldon shook it.

She wrapped her slender fingers around Darius's, and a jolt traveled up his arm and across his chest before spreading heat throughout his body.

How perplexing.

He had kissed Eudora's fingers, grasped their delicate length in his, and even spanned the small of her back with his palm, and not so much as a frisson had twitched anywhere on his body.

"Will you draw up a contract, Lord Darius?" Miss Weldon lifted her cup, eyeing him over the rim.

"No. I believe your word is sufficient."

Her mouth parted. "Oh. Yes, of course it is."

Would her lips taste of coffee?

The idea brought Darius's errant thoughts, tumbling back to the present, and he abruptly sat up, uncrossing his leg and bumping the table.

Startled, Miss Weldon jumped.

Why in God's holy name was he wondering about the taste of Miss Weldon's luscious rosebud lips?

"Yes. Well, I suppose I should go, my lord. When should I bring the books?"

"As soon as you'd like." He would write to his parents tonight and ask them for contributions. "I shall have an area prepared for you. I can arrange for a crate for book returns as well."

"Thank you, my lord." She stood and drew on her gloves. "I promise, you shan't regret your decision."

As long as that obnoxious goose didn't accompany her, Darius wouldn't.

At least, he hoped he would not.

There was still the merest worry that a library within a bookshop would siphon the sales of his books. This venture wasn't a hobby or a diversion. It was his livelihood now.

Why buy books when one could borrow them for free?

But then again, besides the most popular works currently in demand, his store would offer the latest publications, magazines, periodicals, news sheets, and other books. Considering the nearest city lay three hours away by carriage, and his was the only bookshop in the vicinity, Darius hoped book lovers from neighboring towns and hamlets would also flock to his store to buy the latest editions from their favorite authors.

Mayhap patrons would borrow a book and then wish to purchase it or another by the same author.

He supposed he'd have to wait and see how things played out. Plus, he'd only committed to the library for a limited time.

From beneath half-closed eyes, he observed the whirlwind that was Miss Araminta Weldon. He couldn't help but appreciate her gumption and thoughtfulness.

Though her gown was tasteful and the color became her, even Darius, with the fashion sense of a blind goat, recognized the frock was several seasons out of date, and someone, probably Miss Weldon, had let the hem down.

And yet, her comportment and bearing wasn't that of an impoverished wallflower. She exuded an inner confidence, possessed a keen wit, and displayed a strength of character rare in young women—particularly those not birthed into privilege. There was a great deal to admire about Miss Araminta Weldon beyond her pretty face and gently rounded figure.

"The store opens in six weeks, but the grand event is two months away." He walked her to the door. "You should try to attend as many of the functions during the grand opening week as possible, especially the finale. Bring your sisters and the reverend. I think they would enjoy themselves."

A flicker of uncertainty whisked across her face but was gone in the next blink of her expressive eyes. "I shall do my best, my lord. Papa often requires my assistance, and he's not much on social gatherings that the church does not sponsor."

She probably had nothing appropriate to wear to a formal gathering.

Darius laid a hand on her forearm, and she raised a quizzical glance to his.

Green collided with blue, and another scintillating undercurrent pulsed between them.

"My lord?"

"We'll need to show solidarity to the townspeople, Miss Weldon. Assure them we are not competing but cooperating for the good of all."

"I never considered our arrangement anything else." She slung the satchel over her shoulder. "I would suggest acquiring romantic novels. Though many people look down their noses at romantic stories, they are highly popular among women."

"I'll take your advice under consideration." Annoyance battled with amusement until a wry smile ticked his mouth upward. "I suppose you would include Madame Quillheart in that list? Perhaps I'll even ask her to attend the grand opening and read from one of her novels."

Miss Weldon arched a sage eyebrow, though she appeared to have paled the merest bit. "I'm sure she's far too busy to attend a grand opening at a provincial bookstore."

Provincial?

"Is that a challenge, Miss Weldon?"

"You may consider it one, my lord. I doubt you could persuade her to venture to Woodhaven. The incentive would have to be considerable." Then, with a sweep of her outdated skirts, she departed the bookshop with a duchess's regal comportment.

Mother would like her.

So would Althelia, his sister.

He gripped his chin between his thumb and forefinger. Interesting how he already made that determination but still couldn't be as certain about Eudora's reception.

The truth was, he wasn't all that certain about Eudora at all.

Hands planted on his hips, Darius observed Miss Weldon's lithe form and the gentle sway of her hips until she rounded a corner.

"We'll see about your Madam Quillheart, Miss Weldon. I'll wager she'll not refuse an invitation from the Duke and Duchess of Latham."

With that, he strode inside, straight to his desk.

Yes, sometimes having a duke for a father came in quite useful.

FIVE

※

Westbrook's Book & Coffee Emporium

A FORTNIGHT LATER ~ AFTERNOON

Releasing a happy sigh, Araminta adjusted another book on the top shelf, where she had displayed a few of the newer books. She'd nearly unpacked all she owned and the few the townspeople had generously donated to the library.

"Let me help you."

Darius spoke from directly behind her, his melodic baritone washing over her like cool silk. Goose pimples raised along her arms, and she nearly dropped the book she'd just picked up.

She shouldn't have such a strong physical reaction to him. Neither should she be so happy to see him.

"Good heavens, my lord." Laughing, she turned toward Darius. "You startled me. I didn't know you had returned."

He must have come in the back door. The bell above the main entrance would have tinkled had he come in that way.

A roguish smile tipped his lips upward, and Araminta was hard-pressed not to stare at his mouth.

"I've been in my office," he said.

She'd been so absorbed in her task that she hadn't heard him.

Or had she not known of his return because, holding a volume of Lord Byron's satirical poem *Don Juan* as her dancing partner, she had been humming the *Tyrolese Waltz* and swaying about the library section?

Please don't let it be so.

However, the merriment twinkling in his eyes scorched that futile hope to cinders.

Darius had seen her acting the romantic ninny.

Perfectly wonderful.

He took the book from her hand and set it on the shelf.

As the store wasn't open for business yet, it was just the two of them again. Several times over the past weeks, they'd been alone together. A comfortable comradery had sprung up between them, and with each passing day, she anticipated the few hours in the library with increased excitement.

"May I have this dance?" He held out his hand.

She should say no.

To accept was untenable.

Araminta eyed him skeptically, longing to place her hand in his, yet knowing she was ten kinds of a fool if she did.

"I thought you wanted to help, my lord."

Lifting a broad shoulder, he gave her another rakish smile. "After we dance."

This time, she curled her toes in her shoes to prevent herself from rushing into his arms. She glanced at the window. "Someone might see."

"Not if we stay back here." He clasped her hand, drew her nearer, and began humming near her ear.

How could she refuse?

She was only human, after all.

And Araminta wanted to dance with Darius.

More than anything.

They swayed and turned to the music as he hummed. She lost track of time, fully engrossed in the moment. She never wanted this to end. For a few minutes, she could pretend that he was hers...not Eudora's.

"You dance well," he murmured into her ear, his warm

breath causing a shudder to ripple from Araminta's waist to her nape.

"Thank you. So do you."

Dolt. Of course he did.

He was a duke's son.

He'd probably had dance lessons as soon as he could walk.

"I'm glad I agreed to let you have a library in the store." He turned her, and her skirts swished against his Hessians.

"Me too." Good heavens, her conversational skills were positively riveting.

"I've enjoyed your company, Araminta."

At his whispered words, another delicious tremor rippled through her.

If Araminta didn't know better, she might have read more into the simple phrase. She kept her gaze pointed at his firm chin, shadowed with dark stubble, for she dared not meet his eyes.

Darius chuckled, that marvelous masculine rumble deep in his chest that made her want to press her cheek against the wide expanse.

"Is there something on my chin?" he asked, jollity coloring his voice. "Food? A wart?"

At his teasing, she couldn't prevent her gaze from flying upward to meet his amused eyes. "No."

"Ah, that's better." He leaned a couple of inches

nearer. So near, in fact, that she could smell his sandal-wood and spice cologne. "You have the most beautiful eyes."

"Thank you."

But he was wrong.

He had the most beautiful eyes. She could drown in that gaze, the color of the ocean at twilight. And those silver flecks...?

This was madness. Insanity.

Wholly imprudent.

Clearing her throat, Araminta stepped away.

Bereft, her body cried out at the separation.

"I had better get back to work." She clasped her hands before her.

The doorbell chimed, and Darius cast a frustrated look over his shoulder.

"Lord Darius?" came a woman's practiced sing-song voice.

Eudora.

"Yes, perhaps that is wise." He touched Araminta's cheek, a feather's caress, no more. "For now."

Araminta watched him stride away.

How could she possibly work with Darius and keep her feelings hidden? More painful to contemplate was how could she continue to tend the library, knowing that one day he would likely marry Eudora?

SIX

Westbrook's Book & Coffee Emporium

THREE WEEKS LATER ~ MID-MORNING

"Here's a perfect reading nook, girls."

Araminta waited until the twins had gingerly settled into the overstuffed burgundy armchairs with their borrowed books before placing their hot chocolates and napkins on the rosewood side table between the tufted chairs.

Though they were ten years of age, Araminta wasn't comfortable leaving her sisters alone all day, so she had brought them with her.

Sir Waddlesby had tried to accompany her too, the poor thing.

He missed her.

As she herded him into his pen earlier, she'd promised him a pleasant cuddle tonight and a long walk tomorrow morning.

The things she did for that silly goose.

He had objected, and loudly too, his distressed honks gradually turning into sad chirpings. Never had he endured such regular confinement. Pity for his plight cramped Araminta's chest.

Callidora ventured a sip of her chocolate. "'Tis delicious."

Araminta had acquiesced to the twins' pleas for the sweet beverage, an indulgence she could ill afford. However, the girls would spend the next several hours in the store. It didn't seem right not to purchase something, even though the coffeehouse hadn't officially opened.

Darius had finished his final preparations last week and quietly started permitting patrons to peruse the shelves, make purchases, and order coffee and dainties. The store had seen regular traffic too, despite not formally being open.

Five crates of books had arrived a couple of days ago, surprising Araminta, who thought she too was prepared. The crates contained gifts for the library from Darius's parents. Not that she wasn't grateful for the unexpected bounty—naturally, she was.

Although the Duke and Duchess of Latham's generosity quite delighted her, it also added strain to her already over-burdened schedule. It meant additional hours of work cataloging the recent additions, preparing bookplates, and rearranging the shelves she'd already readied. It also meant she had needed to ask Darius for additional shelf space. He could hardly refuse, given his parents' munificence.

Not that he had appeared the least churlish or belligerent. In truth, he'd been nothing but accommodating and kind. So much so that Araminta's doubts about his willingness to help launch Woodhaven's library had evaporated.

When one spent as much time with someone as she had with Darius these past weeks, one either grew to admire or dislike a person.

She assuredly did not dislike his lordship.

No, she'd discovered a kind, generous man with a delightful sense of humor and estimable moral character. Combined with his dashing good looks, even she, a reverend's pious daughter who rarely ever looked at a man twice, took extra care with her appearance.

You are a foolish twit, Araminta Lilianna Emma Weldon.

He is not for you.

Not if Eudora Clarke had her way.

If only Darius knew the real Eudora. The petty, mean,

vindictive girl who flirted and teased and then tossed men aside when someone richer and more influential showed an interest.

How could Araminta compete with Eudora's elegant beauty and petite perfection? Not to mention her beautiful gowns and perfectly styled hair?

It would be best to put aside her growing fascination with the handsome lord.

Far easier said than done. Spending hours and hours with him over the past weeks had allowed a tiny sprout of attraction to take root and blossom into full-blown captivation.

Not that Darius would ever know.

After all, if Araminta could hide her secret identity from her father, she could certainly subdue her emotions for the charming bookshop owner. Mayhap if she told herself that often enough and long enough, she'd convince herself the tarradiddle was the truth.

And fairies clean the pews each Sunday after Papa's sermon.

The idea of Eudora sinking her talons into Darius, winning him over with her false smiles and contrived demureness, made Araminta physically ill.

He deserved better.

He deserved to know the truth.

Tamping down a sigh, she summoned a smile.

"Take care not to spill chocolate on yourselves, the books, or the furniture, please," Araminta gently admonished her sisters. The last thing she needed was for the twins to ruin something before the store opened.

Papa had departed for London last evening and wouldn't be home until tomorrow night, so Araminta had seized the opportunity to finish setting up the library.

Papa's trip had been a godsend.

She could spend all day in the bookshop.

She'd also brought luncheon today, alleviating the need to return to the parsonage for the midday meal.

Laurella caught her tongue between her teeth as she ever-so-carefully lifted the cup and took a hesitant sip. She grinned. "I feel like a grand lady, Minnie."

"And so, you should." Araminta patted her sister's slender shoulder. "Just remember to behave as such."

Araminta's name had been too much of a mouthful for her baby sisters, and Laurella had shortened it to Minnie when she'd begun talking. Usually, one to take her cues from her bolder twin sister, Callidora, had followed suit.

The nickname had stuck.

Callidora brushed her fingertips over the smooth leather-bound cover of the *Swiss Family Robinson*. "Donating so many books was most generous of the Duke and Duchess of Latham. I could scarcely choose which story to read."

"Me too." Laurella nodded eagerly. "When I finish *Gulliver's Travels*, I shall read your book."

"We'll have to make sure no one else has requested it first," Araminta reminded her. "There is a waiting list, and we cannot be selfish."

Although, truth to tell, when she'd spied a copy of *Northanger Abby*, she'd snatched the book for herself and read it in one night, so tantalizing had it been. However, she made a point to return it the very next day.

Her royalties for *Miss Wimple's Marvelous Adventures* still hadn't arrived, which meant she'd had to take on more embroidery work—primarily gloves and linens. While she couldn't help but feel proud of her ability to create lovely treasures for others, it proved disheartening that she could not afford the same for herself, given the considerable cost of silk embroidery thread.

"I'm trusting you to be on your best behavior, darlings." Araminta gave the twins an encouraging smile. "I'll be just around the corner in the library section."

She turned and encountered the spinster Mulbury sisters, Garnet and Opal, seated at a nearby table with cups of steaming tea and a stack of books covered in brown paper and tied with a string between them. Although shrunken and wrinkled with age, the sisters beamed impishly at Araminta.

"Lord Darius's book selection is most accommodating." Garnet's voice quavered and crackled like old parchment paper. "I'm quite beside myself with anticipation."

"You've also collected quite an impressive selection of books to lend, Araminta." A trifle hard of hearing, Opal spoke loudly, her voice carrying to the room's far corners and causing the twins to glance up from their books for an instant. "Well done, you."

"Indeed," echoed Garnet. "Well done. You should be proud."

"Thank you, ladies."

Garnet sent Opal a mischievous glance.

"I imagine it's not *too* difficult managing the library when you have the company of such handsome lords." Garnet blinked innocently. "I believe Lord Darius and Lord Cassius are both unattached. Are they not?"

She knew full well that they were.

Truth be told, everyone in Woodhaven knew, so what was Miss Garnet up to, the sly old bird?

"*Hmph.*" Opal sniffed as she lifted her teacup, then practically bellowed, "That Clarke chit has set her cap for Lord Darius, poor chap. If he's smart, he'll run for the hills. That one will never be content as a bookseller's wife."

Never had a more truthful statement been made.

"Wasn't it just a few months ago," Opal continued, "that the twit set her hat for Sir Elroy Needleman over in Keswick, and everyone had awaited the toll of wedding bells? Then Lord Darius came along, and she discarded poor Sir Elroy with as much care and consideration as rancid tallow."

One of Araminta's sisters giggled.

Araminta cast a furtive glance around. Thank goodness, other than her sisters and Mr. Sherman, no one else heard the dear woman's comments.

Though a budding smile made his mustache twitch, Mr. Sherman—the epitome of discretion—continued placing cups and saucers on a shelf.

"Fiddle faddle and flimflam." Garnet waved her blue-veined hand as if shooing a pesky fly away. "Her mother will never permit a match between Lord Darius and the spoiled chit. Gertrude's aspirations for her daughter are far loftier, even if Lord Darius is a duke's son."

No small truth there.

Poor Darius.

Eudora's greedy, society-climbing mama—might well prevent the match. It wasn't uncommon, even if the situation was unjust and untenable. Though truth be told, Mrs. Clarke generally acquiesced to her daughter's demands, so if Eudora had her heart set on Darius, there was a slim chance she would prevail. But then, wouldn't she be a constant presence at the bookshop where Darius spent his days?

Then why hadn't the self-centered wretch visited the bookstore more frequently?

It had been at least three weeks since she'd put in an appearance—since that day Darius had waltzed Araminta round the library. That didn't mean, of course, that Darius wasn't seeing Eudora elsewhere. Still, one would think if she were hell-bent on marrying Darius, she'd find any excuse to be with him.

He didn't appear to be pining over Eudora, but men didn't wear their emotions on their sleeves. He might well be languishing over her.

Over the past few weeks, Araminta had grown to regard him with something far more powerful and potent than simple appreciation or attraction. Raw and fresh, she could barely acknowledge these feelings to herself, let alone speak of them aloud.

Garnet glanced around to ensure she wouldn't be overheard and added, "From what I've observed of Lord Darius, he's too kind and decent for that shallow, vain, empty-headed nincompoop. I don't believe I've ever seen Eudora read anything more challenging than an invitation to a ball, let alone a book."

Come to think of it, Araminta had never seen Eudora read anything either.

"No," Miss Opal agreed with a vigorous shake of her silvery head, causing her bonnet's profusion of orange and yellow silk flowers to bob and sway as if buffeted by a spring breeze. "His lordship needs a woman who loves books as much as he does."

The elderly matchmaking dears stared at Araminta, their watery, faded blue gazes not the least repentant about their bold insinuation. They might as well have shouted, *Someone like you.*

Quite impossible.

Isn't it?

SEVEN

Still in the coffeehouse

SEVERAL AWKWARD HEARTBEATS LATER

Of course, the notion was utterly ludicrous. Ridiculous. Preposterous. Outrageous. Absurd.

How could Araminta entertain such a nonsensical idea for one second?

Half a second?

She tried to control the flush crawling from her neck, but her heated cheeks revealed she'd failed in her attempt. Thank goodness no one else occupied the coffeehouse, and her sisters remained absorbed in their books.

Even if she and Darius shared a passion for books, he'd only ever interacted with her in a friendly but professional manner.

What about that dance you shared?

It meant nothing. He'd proven that when the minute Eudora arrived, he'd hightailed it to her side.

Araminta secretly agreed with the Misses Mulburys regarding Eudora's intellect.

Her acumen rivaled a turnip's—a very pretty and cosseted turnip, but a brainless root vegetable, nevertheless. It had always been thus. Araminta had known Eudora since childhood, and intelligence was not her strong suit.

What was it Mama used to say?

You cannot turn a sow's ear into a silk purse.

Nor could you turn a dimwit into a scholar or intellectual.

Displeased with her rambling musings, Araminta summoned a benign smile. "Please excuse me. I only have this afternoon to finish unpacking the books the Duke and Duchess of Latham sent."

"Of course, my dear." Garnet's eyes twinkled as she raised her cup to her lips.

Her sister puzzled her already wrinkled brow. "You work too hard, Araminta. Someone so young should enjoy life."

"I enjoy keeping busy." And Araminta did—just not quite as busy as she'd been of late. She still had to finish writing *The Vicar of Langmere's Daughter,* and Mrs. Tenney had commissioned three more pairs of gloves, which meant more late evenings and less time with the twins before bed.

Sir Waddlesby wasn't the only one to suffer from Araminta's overburdened schedule.

After glancing at her sisters and assuring herself they would be fine, Araminta took her leave of the Mulbury sisters and made her way back to the piles of books waiting to be shelved.

As she rounded the corner from the coffeehouse, Darius raised his dark head from whatever he was reading behind the counter and tipped the corners of his mouth upward a fraction into an enigmatic smile.

A quiver of awareness skimmed over her, but Araminta firmly tamped it down, though she couldn't prevent her mouth from bending upward in an answering greeting.

His smile held nothing the least alluring.

It was the polite smile an employer might give an employee.

Nothing more.

If only that weren't the case.

Araminta continued on her way, noting with a practiced eye the customers who meandered about the bookshop.

Two gentlemen, an elderly matron and her middling-age companion, and a young mother with two fresh-faced boys of perhaps six and seven years of age browsed the aisles with awed reverence. The patrons whispered to each other, uttering frequent exclamations of delight as they carefully perused the books that had captured their interest.

As usual, there was no sign of Lord Cassius. He was probably off painting somewhere. He'd told her he had a gallery in Brighton but wanted to support his twin in his business venture and meant to stay in Woodhaven until the grand opening was over.

Araminta found their good-natured, brotherly bantering amusing and charming.

Though she adored her sisters, their age difference didn't lend itself to the same comradery or emotional intimacy. She missed that the most about Mama—the companionship. And someone to share the workload. The twins tried to help, but after all, they were only ten.

Outside, a wagon pulled by a pair of draft horses lumbered past, causing the sun-streaked windows to shake.

Araminta still hadn't decided what to do about the grand opening festivities and Darius's expectation that she would attend them. The notion of squeezing more activities into her already busy life and getting even less sleep made her head spin.

She grazed her fingertips over the handwritten sign listing the library's operating hours, which hung from a rope hooked to a bookshelf at one end. They had affixed a similar sign to the wall near the coffeehouse's entrance at the other end.

Grateful she had the rest of the day to complete the unpacking without borrowers interrupting her task, Araminta slid behind the simple but effective barricade, taking care to insert the braided burgundy and gold rope into the hook behind her.

The bell above the door tinkled as the matron and her companion departed, each carrying a brown paper-wrapped parcel.

From what Araminta had observed, Westbrook's Book & Coffee Emporium appeared to be flourishing. Hopefully, the library would as well. For certain, the book reservation list had grown significantly these past several weeks.

A comfortable silence descended throughout the bookstore, interrupted occasionally by muted voices from the coffeehouse and the *tick-tocking* of the giltwood wall-mounted clock behind the counter.

Humming, Araminta lost herself in unpacking the books and placing them on the shelves. She never dreamed that her little library would contain just over three hundred books.

Those accustomed to extensive libraries would no doubt scoff at Woodhaven's small collection by comparison. Still, the same sense of purpose and accomplishment she'd experienced upon publishing her first novel made her stand a little taller.

For the next hour, the doorbell jingled in a steady rhythm as patrons came and went, and a boy delivered a package.

"Miss Weldon?"

Recognizing Darius's harmonious baritone, Araminta glanced over her shoulder. "Yes?"

Looking entirely too pleased with himself, he lifted a rectangular package. "I took your advice. These just arrived. Ten editions of Madame Quillheart's latest book —*Miss Wimple's Marvelous Adventures.*"

Momentarily dumbstruck, she could only stare, her jaw slack.

Araminta cleared her throat.

"How wonderful. I assure you, you shan't regret it." She waved at her library shelves. "Since we began, people have consistently checked out her first three books, and there is a growing list of people waiting to borrow them."

He lifted one book from the stack and sauntered over to her. "Here. Add this one to the library too."

The bell chimed again, announcing a patron either entering or leaving.

She searched his face. "Are you certain?"

Gentleness crinkled the corners of his eyes, and her tummy flip-flopped in the most disconcerting manner. Yes, indeed, she did very much admire this congenial Darius.

Perhaps a mite too much, which could prove dangerous for her romantic heart.

Unfortunately, though she'd chided herself thoroughly and presented every argument why she could not entertain such fanciful notions, something deep inside her refused to listen to reason. No matter how much she tried, she could not keep her feelings for Darius in check.

"I am quite certain." He lifted a shoulder and gave her an endearingly boyish grin. Her heart did another somersault. "I plan on donating books to the library too."

She must resist—put aside this silly infatuation.

But he is donating books.

How can I?

"That is very generous of you." She accepted the book, the familiar feelings of pride and accomplishment sluicing over her as she grazed her fingertips over the title.

I wrote this.

If only she could share her secret with the world.

With Darius.

Perhaps someday.

Not as long as Papa is a man of the cloth.

"Thank you, my lord."

Cupping his nape, Darius puffed out his lips in a little sigh.

Once more, she noted how the Good Lord had outdone himself when he'd sculpted Darius's kissable mouth.

"I suppose you should call me Darius, and I shall address you as Araminta since we are to work together closely."

Araminta quite liked the sound of that—working together—not addressing him by his given name. Heavens. Papa *would* have an apoplexy.

What would people say?

Daring Madam Quillheart would do it—call him Darius, that is.

But Madam Quillheart wasn't real.

She didn't have to deal with scandal and disgrace.

Nor could Araminta risk even the hint of a scandal. It could ruin everything she had worked so hard for, not to mention what it would mean for her sisters' futures. No, scandal was best left to the pages of her books, where she could control the story and contrive a happy ending.

"I don't think that would be appropriate." Still clutching the book, Araminta shook her head. A rebellious curl slipped loose of her hairpins and pirouetted near her temple.

For pity's sake.

Why couldn't she have inherited Mama's sleek, shiny locks?

Why must she possess Papa's curly hair? He kept his shorn short, but Araminta didn't have that option.

Darius's mouth twitched in amusement, and he gave the errant tress a flick with his finger.

Her breath left her lungs in a whoosh.

"It's only a name, Araminta."

"True. Nevertheless, I must respectfully decline, my lord." Though a little thrill pulsed along her veins at the suggestion. "People might misunderstand and have the wrong impression if we are so informal."

"I should say they would!"

Araminta and Darius jerked their attention toward the aisle behind them.

Eudora Clarke, resplendent in a sea-foam green and ivory walking ensemble, stood there, impatiently tapping her fine leather shoe on the polished wood floor. She looked like she'd just stepped from a fashion plate. Exquisite and poised. A confection of elegance, except for the frown of annoyance distorting her pretty features.

Araminta barely restrained herself from self-consciously smoothing the front of the sensible white apron she wore over her worn gingham gown.

She was *not* jealous.

She was not.

Well, perchance the *teeniest* bit envious. But the very merest, minuscule amount.

Eudora's overly protective mother was noticeably absent—a true rarity.

So much so that Araminta didn't doubt Eudora had contrived to be alone with Darius. Or as alone as she could be in a public venue.

"'Twould be most unseemly for a vicar's daughter to eschew propriety and presume to use a duke's son's given name." Eudora's tone held the chill of an arctic winter.

There was the sharp-tongued harpy she'd been hiding under a demure demeanor.

The cold ire in the haughty gaze she leveled at Araminta could have frozen molten lava. However, when she turned those big brown eyes on Darius, she appeared wounded and delicate, even turning her plump mouth downward into a pout.

How many hours had she practiced that artifice before the looking glass?

What a consummate actress.

Araminta could not regret her uncharitable thoughts.

It was as obvious as night from day what Eudora was really like.

Why couldn't Darius see the truth when it battered him in the face?

"What can you be thinking, Lord Darius?" Eudora asked, laying her palm on his forearm and brushing her hand up and down its length. "Araminta is not worthy of such an honor."

What a hypocrite.

Anger burgeoned behind Araminta's breastbone.

She couldn't use Darius's given name, but Eudora could caress him in public?

Displeasure drew his raven brows together, and something that might've been distaste or scorn turned his navy blue-eyed gaze flinty.

"I assure you, *Miss Clarke*, that if I give someone leave to use my given name, they have earned the privilege."

Araminta shouldn't have grinned at his declaration or, at the very least, only permitted the merest nascent smile. But Darius coming to her defense was truly marvelous, as was observing the flabbergasted expression whisking over Eudora's features.

Regardless, gloating was a sin.

It seemed Araminta had much to repent of tonight, so why did today feel like such a glorious triumph?

"Come, Miss Clarke. Let us make our way to my office, where we can converse privately." Darius's expression remained unperturbed, but censure still flashed in his eyes.

Araminta would bet Sir Waddlesby it wasn't toward her.

That knowledge sparked highly unchristian-like gratification. She'd atone for her pride later. At this moment, she wanted to enjoy the satisfaction of seeing Eudora put in her place.

Eudora's station was no higher than Araminta's, yet she behaved as if she were nobility, and Araminta was a workhouse pauper born on the wrong side of the blanket. Such haughty and superior airs, Eudora and her intimidating mother put on.

La di da.

"May I impose upon you to oversee the bookshop for a few minutes, Araminta?" Darius asked, as if she would be doing him the greatest of favors.

Eudora pursed her pink lips at his deliberate use of Araminta's given name.

"Of course...*Darius.*"

His answering grin could've lit a midnight sky.

Eudora scowled openly, not attempting to hide her displeasure. Her heated glower—meant to incinerate Araminta—merely amused her.

What a petulant, spoiled chit.

Mayhap, the Misses Mulbury were correct.

Darius should know about Eudora's true nature. Although it would be far better if he recognized her shortcomings on his own.

He grasped Eudora's elbow and guided her away but halted after a handful of steps.

"I nearly forgot, Araminta. I think you'll be pleased to know that Madam Quillheart's publisher responded to my invitation for her to join the other authors at the grand opening. They think it is a splendid idea and promised to notify her of the date and time and strongly encourage her to take part. One of her publishers even offered to venture to Woodhaven himself."

Sweet Jesus on Sunday.

Araminta's heart and stomach plummeted to her feet.

What a fine pickle she was in now.

EIGHT

Darius's office

TEN MINUTES LATER

After Darius steered Eudora into his office, taking care to leave the door wide open not only so he could monitor the store but to prevent any suggestion of something inappropriate occurring, he released her elbow.

Arms folded, he rested a hip on the edge of his desk and regarded her.

And he didn't like what he observed.

Furthermore, he couldn't help but compare Eudora's artifice to Araminta's wholesome, unpretentiousness—her kindness and *joie de vivre*—joy of life.

The two women were opposites in nearly every way, from their coloring to their temperament and lifestyle, and his increasing appreciation of Araminta's uniqueness seemed to be in direct proportion to his escalating awareness of Eudora's lack of character.

Thus, a fortnight ago, he'd determined not to pursue Eudora any longer.

They would never have suited, and a union between them would have resulted in mutual unhappiness and, perhaps in time, resentment and animosity.

Thank God he'd discovered that truth before things had gone any further.

Sweet Araminta, who hummed to herself, had a goose for a pet, and loved books as much as he did—had given him a glimpse of true happiness and of the kind of relationship his parents and married siblings enjoyed.

He swept his critical gaze over Eudora.

The epitome of Society fashion and as lovely as he'd ever seen her, Eudora exuded a sullenness and privileged expectancy he'd never noticed before. More fool him, because as certain as he was that the sun would set tonight, those character flaws had always been present.

His infatuation with her beauty had prevented him from seeing who she truly was.

It had taken spending time with Araminta, a woman incapable of artifice, to recognize how shallow and insipid Eudora was.

Thank God he hadn't proposed.

Nor would he.

Cassius had been right—confound his insightful twin.

Eudora Clarke was not the woman for him. Something inside him had whispered that from the very beginning. Mayhap, that was why he couldn't envision her with his family.

"I'm surprised to see you without your mother acting as chaperone, Miss Clarke."

He shifted and crossed his ankles.

Araminta's tinkling laughter carried into his office, followed by Cassius's familiar tenor.

A stab of jealousy rooted around Darius's belly.

He'd never been jealous of his twin before, and he didn't like the sensation.

Tilting her head at a coy angle—another practiced pose—Eudora glided toward him. Her perfume, no doubt expensive and custom-made, wafted upward. "Mama is at the milliner's. She permitted me to stop in the bookshop alone for a few minutes."

"Indeed?" Darius cocked an eyebrow, his intuition on high alert.

Eudora batted her eyelashes and produced a siren's smile. "I've convinced her to allow you to court me."

That took Darius aback.

He'd expected to work much harder to persuade Mrs.

Clarke to view him favorably. Moreover, it had been weeks since he'd actively pursued Eudora.

A month ago, his primary focus had been winning her hand. Now, the idea held as much appeal as eating cold, congealed eggs cooked in bacon grease.

What had changed him so drastically?

Araminta.

She'd literally knocked him over, and he could think of little else since meeting her, including the woman standing before him. That either made him shallow and fickle, or he'd finally regained his senses.

He very much suspected it was the latter.

Eudora sashayed closer and ran a gloved fingertip from his neckcloth to his waistcoat's first button. A seductress's practiced move. She obviously believed she had him wrapped around her little finger, that he'd concede to her every wish and whim.

She had miscalculated.

Tremendously.

"And, how may I ask, did you manage that?" he asked

He was dashed curious to know.

Eudora glanced upward, clearly confident of her physical charms.

"You are a Westbrook, Darius. Mama realized what a powerful, wealthy, and influential family you have. She doesn't even mind that you're so far removed from inheriting the title." Eudora swept her mouth into another artificial smile. "Mama has decided ours would be an acceptable match. Aren't you pleased?"

Did Eudora have any idea how mercenary and condescending she sounded?

"I'm flattered, I'm sure." Sarcasm dripped from each word.

How could he not have seen she was no better than her mother when it came to coveting station, position, power, wealth, and influence?

Still completely oblivious to his derision, Eudora gave him a brilliant smile. "She has a few provisions, mind you—"

I'll just bet she does.

"—but I'm certain the stipulations aren't anything we cannot compromise on," she finished confidently.

Darius scratched an itch at his nape before nodding. "Go on."

"Well..." For the first time, Eudora seemed hesitant, and uncertainty shadowed her features. A moment later, she'd regained her equanimity. "She says if the Latham duchy were to guarantee you a minimum five-thousand-pound allowance annually and provide an estate with paid staff for us, she would permit me to marry you."

Five thousand...?

An estate? With staff?

Sweet Jesus.

What a money-grasping, conniving bit of muslin.

"Is that *all*?" Darius replied in a dry voice, barely keeping the contempt thrumming through him from his expression and tone.

"I knew you'd agree, darling," Eudora purred, still completely ignorant of his pointed and caustic mockery.

She's dense as a parsnip.

Beaming, she splayed both palms against his chest, giving him the understanding that she wasn't the innocent miss she'd pretended to be.

"Naturally, Mama would wish to live with us when she isn't traveling with her companion. I'm positive you wouldn't begrudge her an allowance and her own personal staff."

"You two seem to have worked out all the details—addressed every consideration." He rubbed the bridge of his nose with two fingers.

"Oh, yes. Yes, we have, indeed." A sunny smile lit Eudora's face—a face Darius had once believed the most exquisite he'd ever beheld.

Until Araminta came into his life, that was.

"Do go on," he encouraged wryly, rather enjoying this game of cat and mouse.

Eudora gave an eager nod.

"We've spent months..." She blushed, appearing stricken and guilty. "Oh, dear. I wasn't supposed to share that tidbit."

What a conniving pair.

So the wily Clarkes had spent months baiting him, manipulating him, encouraging him to believe he had to win Eudora's hand when they had no objection to a union all along.

As long as a guaranteed bloody fortune accompanied Darius to the altar.

It made him feel cheap and used.

Did a woman pursued for her dowry feel the same way?

Fury simmered in his veins.

Providence had barely spared him a lifetime of horror with this devious, scheming wench.

"Except for one major problem." He lifted a finger. Then another. "Well, two, in truth."

NINE

A HALF DOZEN UNCOMFORTABLE
HEARTBEATS LATER

Eudora puckered her forehead, seemingly genuinely confused. "No, I don't believe we forgot—"

"First—" Darius didn't let her finish. He had heard enough. "I would *never* presume to ask my father or his heir to guarantee me an annual allowance from the duchy's coffers. It is not my birthright. Besides, I am a man who prefers to make his own way in the world."

"Stuff and nonsense." She pooh-poohed his objection as if he'd suggested she select a Maid of Honor Tart for tea rather than a Shrewsbury. "Your father has oodles of money. It's no secret, Darius. Don't you want to make your bride happy?" she crooned seductively before forming her mouth into a well-practiced moue.

Ah, there was that pout again.

"Mama has vowed she shan't consent to the match otherwise."

Of course, the fortune-hunting dame had.

Eudora curved her lips into a coquette's invitation.

"*Surely* we can negotiate financial requirements, Darius dearest."

Pressing her length against him, Eudora moved suggestively.

Definitely *not* an innocent.

There were names for women like her, and none were the least flattering.

Darius grasped her upper arms and set her away from him.

"The second thing you and your manipulating mother have forgotten is that I have not asked you to marry me, Miss Clarke." He paused for effect, enjoying the moment far more than a gentleman should have done. "Nor do I intend to propose."

"But.... but..." She retreated a step, appearing utterly dazed and confounded. "But you simply must. *Must*, I say!" As if repeating herself would make it a fact. Eyes wide and wild, she gestured frantically. "Everyone is expecting it. *I* expected it!"

Nay, she and her harpy of a mother expected to live out their lives in the lap of luxury, no doubt imposing upon his parents to finance their every frivolous whim.

"No, I *mustn't*." Darius pointed toward the door. "We are done here. You should go."

Narrowing her eyes in a manner that reminded him of a furious cat, Eudora planted her hands on her hips.

All pretense of affability had flown with his rebuff.

"You cannot discard me like an old shoe or a stained handkerchief, Darius Westbrook. I shan't have it." She stomped her foot like a toddler. "I'll claim you violated me."

An unbecoming sneer contorted her face.

She'd best take care, or she'd develop wrinkles from all her scowling.

"You'll have no choice but to marry me then," she declared.

He permitted a mocking half-smile to arch his mouth.

"As this is the first time I've ever been alone with you, Eudora, you know there has never been an opportunity to compromise you. Likewise, as the door is wide open, I'm certain several people in the bookstore have heard every word of this conversation, and no one will believe your madcap fabrications."

She blinked rather owlishly and darted a brief, half-panicked glance at the open door as he stated the inarguable facts.

Hands thrust into his pockets, he leaned forward, rather enjoying her discomfiture.

"I'm sure you don't wish to be shackled to a working-class gentleman your entire life, do you? For I'll not accept a groat from the duchy at your request. As a matter of principle, I shall refuse any help from the current and future dukes. I don't think you'd flourish in impoverishment."

The point was moot, in any event.

No circumstances could compel him to exchange vows with her.

"It's your word against mine, Darius." Eudora lifted her pointed chin in smug defiance. "Who do you think the townsfolk of Woodhaven will believe?"

A formal naval officer who served with distinction and honor and the son of a respected peer of the realm or the pampered, willful daughter of an unpleasant, greedy harpy?

"I think we both know the answer to that question, Eudora," he said, his tone dryer than the Sahara's summer sand.

Worry pleating his forehead, Cassius peered around the doorframe.

Bless the interfering rapscallion.

"Right you are, Dare. I've been blatantly eavesdropping just outside the door." His visage stern, Cassius shifted his attention to Eudora. "Unlike my buffleheaded brother, I never trusted you, Miss Clarke. I recognize a fortune hunter when I smell one."

He wrinkled his nose as one does when one chances upon fish rotting in the afternoon sun on a hot summer's day.

Cassius continued conversationally, as if they sat in Hefferwickshire House's drawing room, exchanging banal pleasantries. "When Miss Weldon informed me that my imbecile of a brother had escorted you to his office, I deemed it prudent to spy unabashedly upon you."

He reached behind him and dragged Araminta into the entrance.

"Using the guise that two witnesses are better than one, I also compelled Miss Weldon to eavesdrop. To her credit, she was most reluctant to intrude." A rather smug grin split his face. "I, happily, have no such compunction."

Darius's usually taciturn twin appeared positively gleeful.

Araminta lifted her contrite green-eyed gaze to Darius's, and he couldn't summon a jot of anger. Their joint testimony would protect him if Eudora carried out her preposterous threat. Though why she would when he'd made it clear that he would probably never possess the amount of money she coveted was beyond him.

"We heard everything as well." Garnet Mulbury

stepped forward, arm in arm with her sister Opal, their eyes alight with mischief. "Safety in numbers and all that."

"'Twas quite entertaining, I must say," Opal added with a cheerful smile.

"Miss Weldon, do forgive our forwardness." Garnet turned to address Araminta. "We took the liberty of purchasing another hot chocolate and more biscuits for your sisters." She leaned in and whispered sotto voce, "Didn't think their young ears should hear this claptrap."

"Thank you." Araminta gave her a grateful smile.

"Where is my daughter?" Mrs. Clarke's imperious voice rang out from the shop floor. "Eu-doooooo-ra?"

Her bellow rose an octave on the last syllable.

Bloody perfect, but not unexpected.

"Where are you, daughter?" Mrs. Clarke called in a sing-song voice. "With your betrothed?"

Several audible gasps carried into the office.

Apparently, everyone in the bookstore had taken it upon themselves to listen in on the conversation, and several had assembled just outside his office.

Good for them.

Darius would emerge from this potential scandal unscathed.

Eudora, on the other hand...

The machinating wench and her meddlesome mother had clearly planned this debacle, and they deserved the unpleasant and likely lasting repercussions.

"Lord Darius is not her betrothed," came the satisfied voice of an older woman.

A male patron chimed in, "Turned the chit down flat, he did."

"Even after she tried to blackmail him," another woman added. "Such a shock. Is that how you raised your daughter, Mrs. Clarke?"

"Do shut up, you cackling hens," Eudora bit out between clenched teeth as she stomped across the floor, fury accenting every step. Gone was the guise of a demure, sweet-tempered, biddable miss. A malevolent, intractable viper had replaced her.

Araminta, Cassius, and the Mulbury sisters slipped farther inside, each giving the frothing female, Darius had once considered marrying, a wide birth.

"I shall *not* be publicly scorned," Eudora fairly snarled each clipped word. "This is not the end of this, Lord Darius."

"Oh, I very much think it is." Cassius quirked a dark eyebrow. "You've no recourse. None. Except, perhaps, to leave town."

Eudora rounded on Araminta and jabbed a finger at her.

Araminta stood her ground, poised and calm.

Brave darling.

"You caused this, Araminta Weldon," Eudora seethed. "I know you have always been jealous of me. You wanted

Lord Darius for yourself, you plain, dowdy, frizzy-haired frump." She pointed her critical gaze at Araminta's gown, then at her bare hands. "You're no lady. Your clothes are hideous, and you don't even wear gloves."

Did Eudora think disparaging Araminta cast her in a better light?

Far from it.

Her unkindness had the opposite effect, as demonstrated by the contempt etched on the face of every person who'd witnessed her outburst.

"I did no such thing, and you well know it," Araminta said in a serene voice. "As for my clothes, yes, I've altered them from kind donations to the church. But clothes do not make a person. Nor do I need to justify myself to you. Furthermore, only a birdbrain would wear gloves while handling stacks of books. They would become irreversibly soiled."

Araminta met Darius's gaze across the room, and for a moment he forgot there was anyone else there. His sister had described that feeling to him—of how she felt when she met Owen's gaze across a crowded ballroom, and everything and everyone disappeared, and they were the only two people in the room.

Magical.

That was how Althelia had described it.

Darius had thought it a silly romantic notion.

Something his dear sister would say, but now, in this moment, he believed her.

It *was* magical.

What's more, he hoped—*prayed*—Araminta felt it too.

She turned her glittering, green-eyed gaze on Eudora.

"Besides, to harbor jealousy, I'd have to envy something about you, Eudora. You've made it plain as day to everyone present that there is nothing inwardly or outwardly the least enviable."

Touche!

Darius barely refrained from applauding.

Cassius clasped his hands behind his back and gave her an approving nod.

The Mulbury sisters did not hide their exuberant grins.

"Someone's getting their comeuppance," Garnet whispered to Opal.

"*Ooh. Ooh*," Eudora hissed, seemingly unable to cobble a coherent response together. "You...you..."

She raised her hand as if to slap Araminta.

"Do not dare!" Darius roared. He was across the room in an instant and stood in front of Araminta, shielding her with his body. "You can direct your fury at me, but no one else deserves your wrath, most especially not Araminta."

Mrs. Clarke trundled into the office, her face as

flushed as a squalling babe's. She looked as if she were about to erupt into a tantrum.

"What is the meaning of this?" Taking a position beside her petulant daughter, she shook her cigar-like finger at Darius. "You've compromised my daughter's reputation. Duke's son or not, you shall do the honorable thing."

Darius scratched the side of his nose.

A gentleman wouldn't utter the words parading through his head. His ungentlemanly impulse would disappoint Mother and Father. Yet sometimes, the truth needed saying.

This was such a time.

"I'll wager a *gentleman* compromised your daughter long ago, but nothing occurred in this office that can be construed as untoward." He canted his head toward the quartet near the doorway. "Ask these upstanding witnesses."

"*Witnesses?*" Mrs. Clarke whispered in a deflated voice as she took in the bystanders.

The Mulbury sisters wiggled their gloved fingers in a little wave. Cassius saluted, and Araminta gave a firm nod.

"Mother, I want to go home," Eudora snapped before shoving past the other enraptured onlookers who had eased into the office. "I told you this wasn't a good idea. Now see where it has led us, you stupid cow? I shall never be able to show my face in Woodhaven again."

Despicable didn't begin to describe Eudora.

An amazingly subdued Mrs. Clarke followed her daughter.

Eudora's true colors hadn't shown until now, and they weren't pretty.

You, Darius Ethan Trent Westbrook, have been spared a lifetime of misery—all because a lovely girl wearing a hideous gown had chased her goose down the street and knocked him off his ladder.

Surely God had a sense of humor.

"Thank you. I don't know how to express my appreciation." Darius scraped a hand through his hair as he took in each onlooker. "Please go about your business. I shall return to the bookshop momentarily."

The spectators shuffled away, murmuring amongst themselves.

Cassius extended an elbow to each Miss Mulberry. "Allow me to escort you, delightful ladies."

"Young scamp." Garnet gave him a cheeky smile.

"Indeed," Opal agreed. "But very charming."

Araminta turned to leave but hesitated at the threshold and gave Darius a searching glance. Compassion softened the gentle edges of her face and radiated from her emerald-green eyes.

"I'm sorry, Darius. That was awful. I know you regarded Eudora highly."

A polite way of saying Eudora's beauty had blinded

him; therefore, he hadn't seen her superficiality or deviousness.

"Yes, it was, but I'm glad I finally saw her true nature." Darius offered a wry grin. "I have you to thank for that."

"Me?" Confusion whisked across her pretty face. "How so?"

"If I hadn't met you, Araminta, I'd never have understood that your inner beauty composed of goodness, kindness, and generosity outshines Eudora as brightly as the sun does a candle."

TEN

THREE DAYS LATER ~ MORNING

Humming as Sir Waddlesby rooted around by her feet, nibbling on succulent spring grass, Araminta hung the laundry to dry. Papa had arrived home the day before yesterday and had taken to his bed with a severe chest cold.

As poor luck would have it, Callidora and Laurella had contracted the illness, though the robustness of youth had reduced their symptoms to sore throats, a slight fever, and a hacking cough.

The twins enjoyed spending a few days in their bedclothes, tucked under a swath of blankets, while they read the treasures they'd borrowed from the town's new library, sipped tepid ginger tea laced with honey, and spooned steaming chicken broth.

With a household of sick people to care for, Araminta had missed her shift at the library yesterday. She'd sent a note round to Darius, apologizing and promising she would return as soon as possible.

Hopefully, he wouldn't presume her absence would become habitual. More often than not, her life was a predictable routine, which perhaps was why working in the library held so much appeal. In point of fact, she wouldn't mind being a clerk in the bookstore either, not that her schedule permitted it.

Neither would Papa.

She still hadn't finished writing her current novel, and the manuscript was due next month. Her publisher had inquired about the story's progress in the correspondence Araminta had received yesterday, along with her royalty payment—a missive strongly suggesting that she attend Westbrook's Book & Coffee Emporium's grand opening event.

Wrinkling her nose, she glanced upward, her attention following a chaffinch's graceful path as the bird flitted to the apple tree on the other side of the parish lawn. Normally, the sweet little birds hopped around beneath the hedgerows.

A gentle breeze tickled the tree's pinkish-white

blossoms.

As she watched, the chaffinch took to wing again, this time landing atop the embattled parapet's corner pinnacle.

She surveyed the timeworn, age-mellowed stones of the ancient parish. She loved this rustic, rubblestone church. Its existence, dating back centuries, was an enduring symbol of strength and constancy to the community, but especially to Araminta and her family.

Saint Andrew's was also the only home she and her sisters had ever known. Papa had no desire to advance his career and move to a larger parish. He vowed he'd die preaching from Saint Andrew's pulpit.

An involuntary sigh escaped Araminta, causing her cheeks to puff out momentarily.

Perhaps it was just as well she had a few extra days to digest Darius's compliment.

Your inner beauty, composed of goodness, kindness, and generosity, outshines Eudora as brightly as the sun does a candle.

Araminta wanted to believe his reverently spoken words meant more than they did—that his break with Eudora wasn't simply because of that woman's devious and avaricious nature. That perhaps he might have feelings for Araminta...

She secured a sheet on the line with a wooden pin.

Tonight, her family would sleep on spring-freshened-air-dried-sun-warmed sheets.

Clean sheets.

One of life's often overlooked blessings.

Had she been of a different temperament, she might've resented being cast into the role of mother to her sisters, hostess for her father, and secret income supplementer. Instead, she accepted her lot and did so with a cheery attitude.

What good would sulking, pouting, complaining, and being an all-around grumbletonian do? Besides, thanks to her late mother's encouragement, she was a bona fide published author. Even though she wrote under a pen name.

Until now, Araminta rarely considered what would become of Papa and the twins should she marry. They relied on her so much. The point was moot as she'd never had a serious suitor—Clarence Button's wholly one-sided infatuation notwithstanding.

But love had awakened her soul—even if the man responsible for rousing her heart from dormancy would likely never know. Still, that didn't prevent her from daydreaming when she should have been sleeping so she wouldn't awaken exhausted the next day. That same foolhardy preoccupation might also be partially responsible for why she'd fallen behind on her novel.

How many times since the day she'd accidentally knocked him off his ladder had she lost herself in woolgathering about Darius?

She'd lost count.

Dare she harbor a tiny hope that he had developed a budding regard for her as she had for him, or was he simply being kind or gentlemanly? Naturally, as a duke's son, one would expect him to have impeccable manners.

Except experience had taught her from occasional interactions with aristocrats in the past, the behaviors and manners of *Le beau monde* usually proved self-serving and condescending at best and downright uncivil at worst.

"Stop it, you gullible goose," she muttered crossly to herself.

Just for reinforcement, she added a couple more self-castigations because entertaining whimsical fantasies was plain stupid.

"Peagoose. Saddle-goose."

"Saddle Sir Waddlesby?" A manly chuckle filtered to her. "I'd like to see that."

What?

She poked her head around the sheet she'd just finished hanging on the line.

A basket covered by a tea towel clutched in one hand, Darius stood there, a wholly disarming smile curving his firm mouth upward.

"Good morning, Araminta."

He addressed her with the ease and confidence of someone who believed it was their right.

"Good morn to you as well."

Why was he here?

"I wasn't expecting you." She nearly rolled her eyes at stating the obvious. Lest he feel unwelcome, she rushed to add, "But I'm glad you came."

Oh, for pity's sake, Araminta.

Now she sounded *too* eager.

Sir Waddlesby waddled over and longingly eyed the black gloves Darius wore.

Ho-onk. Ho-onk.

He offered a muted greeting as he stretched his long neck toward the treasure he so adored.

"Oh, no, you don't, you rascal." Darius chuckled, the warm rumble resonating in his broad chest. "Just a moment, my good fellow. I have something for you."

He glanced upward, his gaze meshing with Araminta's. "I think you will both be very pleased."

He winked, and she forgot to breathe.

Lord, he was devastatingly handsome this morning, his dark blue eyes rivaling the spring twilight. He wore a cobalt coat, black trousers, and an azure and black paisley waistcoat. Though he claimed to be of the merchant class now that he operated Westbrook's Book & Coffee Emporium, no one would ever mistake him for anything but quality.

His facial features and bearing betrayed his noble breeding.

Yet not once had he behaved like an arrogant ponce.

Glancing downward, she hid a grimace.

Planning on spending the day completing chores, she'd slipped on one of her oldest, most worn frocks when she'd arisen at dawn. A gingham yellow floral affair, the gown's once cheery colors had faded into obscure shades and shapes. And worst of all, she hadn't confined her wild hair into a tidy knot but had secured the untamed curls at her nape with a ribbon.

After fishing around in his basket for a moment, Darius withdrew a glove. "When I wrote and asked my parents to send books for the library, I also asked them to collect gloves missing their mate."

Still wearing that distracting grin, he glanced at the basket. "They sent several. How a glove goes missing, I have no idea. Nevertheless, I should think there are enough gloves here to keep Sir Waddlesby happy for a while and prevent him from stealing."

Darius dangled a lady's blue glove for the goose whose black button eyes lit with joy. Issuing a gleeful hum, Sir Waddlesby accepted the offering, then pelted through the rose and vegetable gardens with his treasure hanging from his mouth.

"Thank you," Araminta said in an unfamiliar breathless tone. "Sir Waddlesby is as happy as he's ever been."

"You're welcome." Huskiness deepened Darius's voice.

Observing her beloved goose clicking and humming to

himself in complete delight, she offered Darius a tremulous smile. If she hadn't already fallen head over heels in love with Darius Westbrook, his thoughtful gift certainly clinched it.

No one had ever done anything as kind and thoughtful for her, let alone her mischievous pet. She had no doubt that Sir Waddlesby would follow Darius about like a devoted puppy now, which meant the bookstore might well have a regular feathered visitor.

"That was very thoughtful of you, Darius."

They stared at each other in silence for a few lengthy moments until she remembered where they were.

Glancing swiftly over her shoulder at the parish cottage, she said, "Papa and the girls aren't in a state to receive visitors, but I made shortbread this morning and could offer you a cup of tea to go with it." She pulled a face. "I know you prefer coffee, but I'm afraid we don't have any. Papa's a tea drinker to his core."

"I'd like that very much." The smoldering smile Darius gave her nearly unhinged her knees. "I've brought books for the twins and your father and seed cake, pasties..."

No other parishioner had brought so much as a spoonful of honey to soothe sore throats, let alone the bounty that Darius carried.

He gave the basket a rueful glance before shrugging. "Truthfully, I'm not exactly sure what Mr. Sherman put in here. I told him to fill it with food to tempt one's appetite. I think there's a custard too."

"That was most considerate of you. I'm sure Papa and the girls will be thrilled." After bending and retrieving the laundry basket, Araminta angled toward the kitchen entrance. "Shall we?"

"Certainly." Darius fell into step beside her.

Silence stretched between them, poignant and titillating.

With every step, Araminta became more aware of his masculine charisma. It didn't help that the muscles in his thighs bunched with each stride he took. She floundered for something to say to distract her from the far too virile man beside her.

"You needn't have made a special trip just to deliver the gloves to Sir Waddlesby. You could have waited until my next shift at the library."

Except he'd also brought food for her ailing family too. *Nincompoop.*

"I could've waited, but I wanted to see you, Araminta. I've thought of little else these past few days."

There was that husky tenor again, sending a wave of awareness cascading over her.

She stumbled but recovered her balance.

Not, however, before he made a rough sound in his throat and cupped her bare elbow. Though he wore gloves, a streak of electricity zipped up her arm to her shoulder, across her back, and straight to her heart.

Behind them, Sir Waddlesby released muffled hums and honks, the glove still clenched in his beak.

Just outside the open kitchen door, Araminta paused and, summoning her courage, met Darius's penetrating gaze. Warmth and tenderness emanated from his eyes. But something else simmered in those blue depths.

Something more potent.

"Why have you been thinking of me?" Goodness, there she went, sounding breathy again.

"Because, my darling," his expression grew impossibly more tender, "I've fallen hopelessly, irreversibly, and completely in love with you."

A proper lady would've reacted with demureness and restraint, but what proper lady owned a pet goose and wrote romance novels?

Instead, Araminta dropped her laundry basket, almost hitting poor Sir Waddlesby on the head.

He gave a startled *honk* before sidestepping several paces.

She threw her arms around Darius's neck and clung to him, not caring that anyone might come along and see her. "I didn't dare hope you loved me too."

Darius encircled Araminta's waist with his free arm and pulled her so near their thighs brushed. Then his lips were upon hers, and time stopped as sensation and desire encapsulated her.

Who knew a tongue could cause such arousal?

Such compelling need?

Her blood sang in her veins as her heart thundered with untold happiness.

"I hope you intend to propose to my daughter, Lord Darius."

Papa!

Darius lifted his head but didn't release Araminta. He turned toward her father, still holding her close to his side. "Yes, sir. I do. With your blessing."

Wearing a navy blue quilted banyan, Papa appeared to have recuperated overnight. His expression was kind but serious as he shifted his focus between Araminta and Darius.

"I needn't ask if you love him, daughter." Papa smiled, a hint of mirth in his eyes. "It's been obvious as a pig wearing a tartan and a tiara that something has been distracting you." He shifted his focus to Darius. "Or rather, *someone*."

Unable to subdue her smile any more than she could the riot of curls on her head, Araminta nodded.

"I do love Darius, Papa."

"Well, then. I suggest you come inside, my lord." Her father stepped aside. "We can discuss a date, though I'd guess you'll want to wed as soon as I have read the banns thrice."

"Indeed, sir." Darius dropped his loving gaze to her. "If you are agreeable, Araminta."

Araminta's pulse stuttered.

So soon?

What would become of Papa and the girls?

Who would take care of them?

Her concern must have registered on her face.

"I see your hesitation, daughter, and I can guess the cause." Papa rubbed his chin. "I mean to hire a housekeeper and governess. My meeting in London went extremely well, and the Church has raised my annual compensation considerably."

As the Church should have done over a decade ago.

Relief washed over Araminta. She slid her hand into Darius's warm palm. "It won't be too much with the grand opening? We could wait until afterward."

She didn't want to wait, but Darius had been planning the bookstore's opening for months.

"Not at all." Shaking his head, he touched her cheek. "My family is coming for the grand opening. Now they'll have something else to celebrate while they are here. Trust me. They'll be thrilled. We'll have to postpone our honeymoon for a few months, though."

"I don't mind." Certain she'd never been happier in

her entire life, tears pooled in Araminta's eyes. "Then three weeks it is."

ELEVEN

Westbrook's Book & Coffee Emporium
Grand Opening

JUNE 1828 ~ NEARLY MIDNIGHT

Had a mortal ever been this happy?

Darius glanced down at his wife of two days. Stunning in an emerald-green gown with a shimmering overskirt that changed colors when she moved, she fairly took his breath away.

Mama's lady's maid had tamed Araminta's curls into an elaborate coiffure from which three artfully placed peacock feathers perched. A wedding present from his parents, an emerald pendant nestled between her breasts, and matching teardrop earrings hung from her dainty earlobes.

Several ladies had exclaimed in awe over her elaborately embroidered white elbow-length gloves and asked where she had acquired them. However, Araminta's days of embroidering for a commission were over. In the future, she could use her talent because she wanted to, not because she had to.

The strains from the string quartet his mother had arranged drifted into the bookstore from the coffeehouse as guests waited for the next author to read an excerpt. Many more patrons stood around the perimeter, and there wasn't an unoccupied spot anywhere in the store.

"I'd say your grand opening is a rousing success." Having already shared from one of his travel books, Leonidas had removed his mask. He slapped Darius's shoulder. "Congratulations, little brother."

To Darius's surprise, Layton had arrived in Woodhaven in time for the wedding. He'd sold his commission in His Majesty's Army and, for the first time since his youth, was free to come and go as he pleased.

Layton winked at Araminta. "All set, Lady Westbrook?"

Darius looked between them, then glanced at Cassius, who had never looked smugger.

Leonidas had a cunning gleam in his eyes too.

What went on here?

"Yes, I am, Layton." Araminta inhaled a slightly unsteady breath, then laid her hand on Darius's arm. "Do you trust me?"

With his life. "Always and forever, my love."

"Have a seat by Papa, please," she said. "He may need moral support in a few minutes."

Moral support?

"Where will you be?" Darius brushed her shoulder with his fingertips. Married just two days, he couldn't get enough of touching her.

"It's a surprise." She fairly sparkled with suppressed excitement.

As Layton and Leonidas led her away, Darius joined his father-in-law.

Given the late hour, Araminta's sisters hadn't attended. It came as no slight surprise that Reverend Weldon had come. Araminta said her father wasn't inclined to participate in social events outside church.

A puzzled frown wrinkled the reverend's forehead as Darius settled into a chair beside him.

Grandmama sat on the reverend's other side, chatting happily with Opal Mulbury.

"Where is Araminta?" his father-in-law asked.

"She and my brothers had something they had to do," Darius said.

On cue, the orchestra music faded away, and the Duke

and Duchess of Latham stood together to announce the next author.

His parents exchanged a glance, their eyes glowing with suppressed eagerness.

Did everyone in his family know something he didn't?

"The program does not list our next guest author because we wanted to keep it as a surprise." The duke caught Darius's eye and grinned. Actually grinned. "Tonight, we have the privilege of welcoming Madam Quillheart."

A collective gasp echoed around the crowded room.

Darius's mother, whose smile could have lit the entire street, continued the introduction once the audience had calmed down. "Madam Quillheart has authored four romance novels, and she plans to publish her fifth early next year. Please join us in welcoming Woodhaven's very own Madam Quillheart."

All heads turned in expectation toward the coffee-house from whence the other authors had entered.

The wall clock rang out, announcing midnight was upon them.

Araminta, flanked by Cassius and Leonidas, stood at the entrance.

Guests and patrons craned their necks for a glimpse of Madam Quillheart.

Leonidas gave Araminta an encouraging smile before Cassius murmured something and passed her a book.

It finally hit Darius then.

Why hadn't he seen it before?

His wife. His beloved, beautiful, brilliant Araminta was Madam Quillheart.

A murmur began and rose in volume as she glided toward the podium, the epitome of grace and confidence.

"I knew it!" Grandmama cried. Gifted with the second sight, Darius's grandmother likely had known Araminta's secret. Beaming, she gave Araminta an exuberant smile. "A girl after my own heart."

Unlike the other authors, Araminta wore no black domino over her face, but this unmasking was even more potent because of who she was.

"Good evening, ladies and gentlemen." She roved those incredible green eyes over those assembled. "I am Madam Quillheart. Please permit me to read a selection from *Miss Wimple's Marvelous Adventures*."

Darius cast a worried glance toward the reverend, who appeared remarkably composed despite the shocking revelation.

Reverend Weldon angled his head, a half-smile arching his mouth. "I knew, you know. Her mother told me on her deathbed."

"Well, *I* didn't, and I'm her husband." Darius couldn't decide if he was more miffed than ecstatic. He focused on his lovely wife, as she finished reading her excerpt.

"Hermione gazed into Palmer's brilliant blue eyes. Without a doubt, she'd fallen, hopelessly, head-over-heels in love with the roguish explorer, Captain Palmer Whitaker.

"'Are you ready for your next adventure, Miss Hermione Wimple?'" He gave her a devilishly charming grin as he lifted her hand to his mouth and grazed his hot mouth over her bare knuckles.

"Nodding, Hermione wrapped her arms around his strong neck. "Oh, I think being your wife will be my grandest adventure yet.'

"THE END."

Araminta finished to resounding applause.

Smiling to himself, Darius made his way to her, having to elbow through a throng of admirers and well-wishers.

No wonder she'd been so keen on him stocking Madam Quillheart's books.

When he reached her side, she gave him an uncertain glance. Before he could tell her how proud he was of her, she said, "I wanted to surprise you."

"Surprise me, you did." He chuckled. "I presume you had to confide in my rascally brothers to pull it off."

"I did." She looked so contrite that he couldn't begrudge her secrecy. "And your parents too. It was past time I revealed who Madam Quillheart was. I am proud of the romances I write."

A flash of defiance sparked in her eyes.

"As well you should be." Darius maneuvered her away

from the crowd. "I didn't know I'd married a famous author."

"You didn't. You married me, a woman who loves you beyond words."

Darius leaned wickedly near to whisper in her ear. "Madam Quillheart? Should we undertake vital research for your next novel?"

She widened her eyes in artificial shock.

"Good sir. Are you suggesting something scandalous? In public, no less?"

"Oh, I am, my love. I am."

And in front of his family, her father, Woodhaven's elite, and everyone else who had packed into Westbrook's Book & Coffee Emporium, Darius swept her into his arms and kissed her like a man long-starved.

"I'll bet she writes that into her next novel." Cassius laughed, and the rest of the guests joined in his merriment.

Araminta opened her eyes and, leaning back in his arms, gave him a saucy wink. "Oh, I definitely shall."

EPILOGUE

Librairie Galignani
Paris, France

MAY 1829

Araminta could scarcely calm the hoard of butterflies flitting around her belly. How could it be that less than a year ago, she'd revealed her identity as Madam Quillheart, and today, she was reading an excerpt from *The Vicar of Langmere's Daughter* at the infamous Librairie Galignani?

In an attempt to subdue the butterflies into submission, she smoothed her gloved hands down the front of her ice-blue gown as she studied the bookstore's charming architecture.

"Nervous?" Darius murmured near her ear.

Mustering a nascent smile, she nodded. "Taut as a bowstring."

"You needn't be, darling." He rested a wide palm on the small of her back in a comforting gesture. "You are a gifted author."

His reassurance calmed her to a small degree.

Now the butterflies merely floated around her belly instead of careening.

"You have to say that." She gave him a cheeky grin. "I'm your wife."

He grazed his palm over her spine and a familiar shudder of desire washed over her.

"I but speak the truth," he said. "I've no doubt you'll be splendid."

Araminta couldn't help but wonder if every author experienced a fit of nerves before a reading. She had that long ago night in Woodhaven when Madam Quillheart had first been revealed, and that was among people she'd known most of her life. Here, in Paris, she knew no one, other than her gracious hosts whom she met only yesterday.

When the owners of the oldest English bookstore outside of Britain had invited her to be a guest, Darius had insisted it was the perfect opportunity for them to also enjoy a long over-due honeymoon. The fact that the Duchess of Latham was a girlhood friend of Giovanni

Galignani's English wife, Anne Parsons-Galignani, might've prompted the unexpected invitation.

Nevertheless, Araminta was over the moon.

Not only was she to tour France, but she'd became a well-known author.

Westbrook's Books & Coffee Emporium had become so successful, that Darius now employed three full-time book clerks, an accountant/secretary, and two additional waiters besides Mr. Sherman.

She peeked at her beloved husband from beneath her lashes.

How could she possibly love him more today than when she'd married him?

Not only were they blissfully happy, they'd achieved success in their chosen professions, and around Christmas, they would welcome a child into the world.

Darius didn't know that tidbit yet.

She would tell him soon.

He smiled down at her, his vivid blue eyes brimming with love. "You are particularly beautiful today, my love. That color is very becoming on you."

"You are quite striking yourself, husband."

Skimming her gaze over his masculine form, she permitted a possessive smile. Even attired entirely in unadorned black, he drew feminine attention like moths to a flame. At this moment, three ladies attired in what must be the latest French fashion stared quite boldly at him.

"I am not the only woman who thinks so."

Araminta directed a pointed look toward the ladies whispering near a table upon which an attractive book display had been arranged.

Darius glanced over his wide shoulder, and instead of blushing or glancing away, the trio gave him seductive smiles.

Araminta tightened her mouth.

Brazen hussies.

Darius must have seen her reaction, for he drew her nearer.

"I only have eyes for you, Araminta, and only shall have for as long as I breathe."

She loved him so much that sometimes it hurt.

"And I, you, Darius."

When his focus drifted to her lips, Araminta didn't hesitate but lifted her mouth for his kiss. This was France after all. Public displays of affection weren't frowned upon quite as much as in England.

Darius settled his warm lips upon hers, and all her qualms and worries drifted away.

"*Ahem.*" A discreet cough directly behind him made Darius lift his head.

Wearing a broad grin, Giovanni Galignani stood there. "We are ready for you, Lady Westbrook."

"Are *you* ready, Araminta?" Darius searched her face, tiny worry lines creasing the corners of his eyes.

"Yes. I am."

No matter what happened, with him by her side, Araminta could withstand anything.

I hope you enjoyed
UNMASKED AT MIDNIGHT
and following the romantic journey
of Darius and Araminta.
If you'd like to leave a review please
scan the following QR Code.

FREE PREVIEW

BOOK 9 ~ CHRONICLES OF THE WESTBROOK
BRIDES
MEMORIES MADE AT MIDNIGHT©

Highbury House
Home of the estimable but dour Earl of Highbury
Brighton, England

AUGUST 1828—EARLY MORNING

Something doesn't feel right...

Singing *Greensleeves* softly to herself, Beatrice Fairfax casually glanced around as she wandered toward her private sanctuary like she did every morning before breaking her fast.

Nothing appeared out of the ordinary, and yet...

Something felt off, as if the day portended unexpected or unpleasant happenings.

A shudder skittered up her spine, and she squinted toward the house.

Yes.

There on the first floor.

Uncle stood before the mullioned study window, observing her, his expression unreadable at this distance.

How peculiar.

He rarely rose before ten.

What prompted him to do so today?

As if sensing her perusal, Uncle Cedric spun from the window and disappeared from view.

Who knew what motivated Cedric Fairfax, Earl of Highbury?

God knew Beatrice had given up trying to understand or please him long ago.

Accompanied by her two canine shadows—Nala, the badly beaten boarhound Beatrice had rescued two years ago from a drunken sailor and who now weighed more than Beatrice, and tiny Teddy, the blind-in-one-eye starving black Pekinese runt she'd found wandering Brighton's streets a few months before that—Beatrice resumed her short trek to what once had been the carriage house.

Waiting for her as he did every morning, Hans, the cook's grandson, waved. He adored helping Beatrice with the animals and wanted to become a veterinarian.

At present, only a few animals called the pretty little

structure, outer cages, and fencing surrounding the building on two sides their home. The sanctuary had also served as a makeshift hospital for many other unfortunate creatures over the years.

An involuntary sigh escaped her.

If only women could become veterinarians.

They couldn't, of course.

Most especially nieces to nobles.

Regardless, that didn't stop Beatrice from reading everything she could get her hands on about the subject. Maybe someday, women would have the same opportunities and rights as men, but that day most assuredly was not today.

And unquestionably would not occur soon.

Not if Uncle Cedric and other stodgy peers had their imperious way.

She'd rescued all her beloved pets, returning to the wild those who could survive in their native habitats and diligently caring for those who could not. They were her dear friends and companions, every bit as loyal as Esme Dawkins and Charlotte Hawthorne—Reverend Ellison Dawkins' eldest daughter and widowed Mrs. Clementine Halsey's only granddaughter, respectively.

Esme and Charlotte didn't care about Beatrice's occasional stutter or her illegitimacy, nor did they judge her for something she had no control over. Their unconditional acceptance and love kept her stoic and determined. They even helped with her menagerie from time to time.

Unlike Uncle Cedric.

The haughty curmudgeon disapproved of Beatrice's interest in animals.

In truth, he disliked everything about Beatrice: her out-of-wedlock birth to his younger sister, her anxiety-caused awkwardness and stutter, her shocking hair, her lack of suitors, and mostly her imposition these past two decades upon his bachelor lifestyle.

Even her name, Beatrice Blossom Carina Fairfax, vexed him. Particularly Carina, because, despite her already married Italian lover's perfidy, Mama had given Beatrice an Italian middle name, meaning beloved.

Uncle Cedric's long nose twitched and his once hand-some features became impossibly sterner whenever Beatrice's friends addressed her by her nickname, *Be Be*.

'Twas what Mama had called her, and Beatrice didn't give two flicks' of a lamb's tail if it annoyed Uncle Cedric into apoplexy. She would not give up the moniker. In that small way, she rebelled against his inflexible strictures. However, in her mind, a riot of recalcitrant thoughts entirely unbefitting a docile, biddable young woman tumbled continually about.

How shocked and appalled would Uncle Cedric be if he had any notion?

Small wonder he permitted Beatrice her pets. But then

again, her animals kept her occupied, and she needn't accompany him to social events they regularly received invitations to.

She was no fool.

Beatrice knew full well her name on an invitation was obligatory, not a genuine desire for her presence. She was an undesirable from her birth on the wrong side of the blanket, to her unpopular coloring, to her propensity for clumsiness and stuttering.

Tending her animals also meant she wasn't in the house and underfoot, exasperating Uncle Cedric at every turn. And as she used her allowance from her trust fund to finance her *little hobby,* as he called it, he couldn't squabble about the expense of her venture, either.

Only two and a half more years—when Beatrice reached her fifth and twentieth birthday—and the bulk of her inheritance would be hers. She could—*and would, my Jove*—leave her severe, unloving uncle's house. At last, she would be free of his censure, dark glowers, cutting retorts, and haughty disdain.

As a child, his callousness and contempt had frightened and discouraged Beatrice. She tried—desperately and pathetically—to earn a smile or a kind word. However, she'd long since stopped trying to gain his approval—an impossibility because of her mere existence and she'd come to accept that fact without rancor.

In truth, at two and twenty, she could leave Highbury

House now, but how did a respectable woman with few marketable skills and no money survive in a world where both were required?

No, Beatrice would bide her time as she had these past years, steer clear of Uncle Cedric as much as possible, ignore his ever-increasing frequent and bold suggestions that she should marry (men weren't exactly lining up to court her), and plan for the day when she was free to make her own decisions.

A refreshing breeze bearing the faintest tangy tinge of the sea caressed Beatrice's face and bare arms. The mild wind flirted with the few remaining purple crepe myrtle blossoms and Persian silk pink pom-poms and also ruffled Teddy's raven fur.

Beatrice had eschewed a bonnet and shawl in favor of soaking in a few rays of glorious sunshine. Soon enough, England's gray, dank, and cold autumn and winter would be upon the coastal township and she would be glad of the indulgence.

How she longed to travel to milder, warmer climes.

She lifted her face skyward—half in defiance and half in indulgence.

What were a few more freckles?

Besides her strawberry blond hair—far more berry than blond—nature had seen fit to pepper her body and face with reddish-brown spots, too many to count. She knew, for more than once as a child, Beatrice had tried to count the imperfections speckling her body.

How cruel the other girls at school had been, poking fun at her spots, pretending they might catch a disease from her.

Lifting her boxy nose, Nala sniffed the air.

Fluffy ears raised, Teddy followed suit before issuing a single *woof*.

The dogs sensed it too—something *was* afoot.

Slowing her pace, Beatrice scanned the landscape.

Other than a pair of turtle doves soaring toward a Katsura tree, nothing disturbed the morning's tranquility. A lone, pristine white cloud floated in the cerulean sky. A ten-foot weather-worn stone wall encased the estate, assuring that no vagrants or uninvited visitors could enter the earl's immaculately tended property.

"It's all right," she assured the dogs, although she wasn't positive everything *was* all right.

Nala gently nudged Teddy's nose and received a wet tongue across her muzzle in response.

Perhaps having both experienced abuse and deprivation, the two dogs had become inseparable, besides being Beatrice's most ardent protectors. She could walk nearly everywhere in Brighton unchaperoned—which she did at every opportunity, despite her uncle's disapproval, though he hadn't forbidden her jaunts.

After all, what was he to do?

Accompany her or forbid her sojourns and bear her presence all the more?

No, permitting her to roam at will was the lesser of the three evils, and how she relished that small jot of freedom.

With her faithful dogs at her side, no one dared so much as glance in her direction without the appropriate degree of respect awarded to the Earl of Highbury's niece.

With another small sigh, Beatrice surveyed the lavish grounds.

Golden sunlight bathed the tidy verdant lawns, neat-as-a-pin hedgerows, the dual rows of meticulously tended roses, and the ostentatious five-story manor painted a pleasant ivory shade.

Elegant stone Grecian urns brimming with trailing ivy and seasonal flowers, including regal orange, pink, red, and yellow begonias, nasturtiums, and a rather new bloom to England, pink and purple petunias, adorned the terrace on the house's west-facing side.

The continuous muffled roar of the waves breaking along the shore echoed in the distance, along with the ringing cries of five gull species.

How Beatrice loved those comforting sounds. She always wanted to live near the ocean, her whole life long, but not in Brighton where she might encounter her uncle.

Filling her lungs with balmy air, she closed her eyes and willed her topsy-turvy stomach to settle. The house and grounds were nothing but a façade, an outward veneer presented to the public and hid the dysfunction inside the elegant residence.

Hans bobbed his blond head as he patted Nala's back. "Morning, Miss Beatrice."

"Good morning, Hans."

He opened the door, and Beatrice slipped into the carriage house, Nala and Teddy on her heels.

Fabian, a three-legged fox, missing half an ear and also blind in one eye, lifted his head and gave her a foxy smile before burying his face in his bushy, russet tail once more. He'd spend this afternoon outdoors in the long run built on one side of the carriage house.

"Can I feed Fabian today?" Hans adored the fox.

"Of course you can."

Sporting a wide grin, the boy hurried to the shelf where Beatrice kept Fabian's food—generally leftovers that the boy's kind-hearted grandmother saved for the animals.

Monty, a hare Beatrice had rescued from a snare, hopped to the side of his cage to greet her, his gait lopsided. Isabella, a dove with a broken wing who would never fly again, but who spent her mornings in an aviary when the weather permitted it, cooed softly. Deaf and blind after two rotten brats had tried to drown him, Lancelot, the ugliest cat Beatrice had ever seen, unfolded from his feline coil and unerringly found his way to her despite his sensory deficiencies.

Laughter bubbled up from her chest at the warm greetings from her animal friends.

Hans chuckled while petting the contented fox, happily munching away on a meaty bone. The lad knew the daily routine so well he could care for her pets all by himself if needed.

Mewing softly, Lancelot wound between her ankles before nudging noses with both dogs. Despite her massive size, Nala was unerringly gentle with the smaller creatures.

"I know you're hungry, my dears. I shall hurry."

After securing an apron over her simple but pretty yellow gingham frock, Beatrice set about tending to her current charges.

She resumed singing as she completed her daily chores, allowing her mind to wander to a time when she'd be free of this gilded prison. Except for eight extremely painful years spent in boarding and finishing schools, awful, humiliating experiences she preferred to put from her mind, Beatrice had never left Brighton.

She fully intended to rectify that once she gained her freedom. Naturally, Nala and Teddy would accompany her. As for her other pets, she planned on hiring someone to care for them while she traveled from one splendid, *warm* location to another.

Surely, if she economized, dedicated herself to thriftiness, and invested wisely, her inheritance could sustain her throughout her life.

Wrinkling her forehead, she paused in sweeping the floor.

She needed to find someone reliable and honest to help her with investing her inheritance.

But who?

Would Reverend Dawkins know of anyone?

It couldn't hurt to ask, but there was no rush. Neither was there any harm in educating herself on the matter, so that when she came into her inheritance, she would be prepared.

The door swung open, and she barely suppressed a gasp.

Uncle stood silhouetted in the opening.

Even at seven and forty, he presented a fine figure of manhood. Tall and slender, he turned many a woman's head. Regardless, he gave no female more than a passing glance. He spent far more time on his toilet and appearance than Beatrice ever had, and she thought him a rather vain man.

Only once before had he ventured into Beatrice's private domain.

Mouth turned down in disapproval, he raked his steely gaze over her, Hans, and the animals.

When had he never spared her a kind word or glance?

Hans sent her a nervous glance before edging toward the doorway. "I'll see you this evening, Miss."

Uncle stepped aside, and the child darted out.

"I've arranged to have an artist paint a miniature of you, Beatrice. I've also purchased a gown worthy of your station for you to wear and have directed Millborn to style your hair." Uncle Cedric gestured toward his own neatly combed rich brown locks tinted at the temples peppered with distinguished gray. "You shall wear my mother's emerald and diamond parure set. I expect you to be ready at half of three when he arrives."

As was his wont, Uncle Cedric gave orders. He never inquired what Beatrice might want or prefer.

Canting her head, she wiped her hands on her apron.

"What n...need is there for me t...to have a m...miniature painted?"

She didn't fool herself into believing it was because he wanted a token to remember her by. This man had rid the house of every single remnant of his sister when she'd eloped with the Italian lace merchant who later broke her heart and left her with child. To this day, Uncle Cedric refused to speak Mama's name, referring to her as "your mother" or "my sister."

"It's enough that I decree it, Niece," he snapped.

His features shifted, and something akin to chagrin flitted across his stern visage, but the impression was so fleeting that Beatrice thought she must have imagined it.

He stepped outside and in his usual unapologetic and arrogant air said, "I've decided it's past time you marry. I mean to travel to London with the miniature to assure potential suitors you are not unbecoming. Once a match has been arranged, you shall exchange vows in London as well."

"M...m...marry?"

Please, God. He cannot be serious.

Would her husband take possession of her money?

She'd never seen the will or trust documents. Neither did she know if her inheritance remained under her control after marriage.

If not...

Beatrice would be in exactly the same position as now.

No, far, *far* worse.

Marriage was for a lifetime. She'd have no hope of escape.

"With your grandmother's inheritance as enticement, even your stutter and lack of social graces might be over-looked, and an acceptable match is not beyond hope." He flicked a piece of lint off his expensively tailored jacket.

He might've requested the butler refold his news sheets, so disinterested did he sound.

She clasped her hands together until her fingertips grew numb. "Am I t...to have n...no choice in t...the m... matter?"

God, how she hated her stuttering.

"Of course, you have a choice." His flinty, gray, emotionless gaze pierced her as he slid his mouth upward an inch into a predatory smile. "You are free to refuse my decree. However, do so, and I shall put you from my house at once. I've met my obligation to your mother."

I hope you enjoyed this FREE PREVIEW of
MEMORIES MADE AT MIDNIGHT
Book 9
Chronicles of the Westbrook Brides Series.
If you'd like to keep reading please
scan the following QR Code.

SCAN HERE TO GET "MEMORIES MADE AT MIDNIGHT"

FROM THE DESK OF
COLLETTE CAMERON®

Woodhaven is a fictional township in Cumberland (today known as Cumbria). Many of Woodhaven's characteristics are similar to Whitehaven, but I didn't want to have to adhere to Whitehaven's historical accuracy. Creating a fictional town allowed me to include the elements of Whitehaven I wanted and still create a unique setting for the story.

A St. Andrews church exists at Sedbergh in Cumbria, but I placed a church with the same name in my imaginary village for this story.

The authors Araminta mentions at the beginning of this story were romance novel pioneers. Their efforts can be partially credited for the popularity of romance novels today.

Librairie Galignani is truly the oldest English bookstore outside of the United Kingdom.

Hugs,

Collette Cameron®

GIGGLES ARE GUARANTEED

If you love to chat about all things romance-book related and enjoy taking part in fun and engaging live events, contests, and giveaways join **Collette's Chèris VIP Reader Group,** my exclusive private book group on Facebook.

Giggles are guaranteed!

Hope to see you there,

Collette Cameron®

Please scan the following QR Code to join:

You Are Cordially Invited To Join

COLLETTE'S THERIS

VIP READER GROUP

ALSO BY COLLETTE CAMERON®
BLUE ROSE ROMANCE® LLC

COLLETTE CAMERON'S®

COMPLETE BOOK LIST

CHRONICLES OF THE WESTBROOK BRIDES
A Romantic Opposites Attract Mystery & Suspense
Family Saga Regency Romance

Moonlight Wishes and Midnight Kisses — Bonus Novella

Midnight Christmas Waltz — Book 1

Mission at Midnight — Book 2

The Midnight Marquess — Book 3

Holly, Mistletoe, and Midnight Snow — Book 4

The Wallflower's Midnight Waltz — Book 5

Minuet at Midnight — Book 6

Kiss a Rake at Midnight — Book 7

Unmasked at Midnight — Book 8

DUKES COME CALLING

A Sensual Marriage of Convenience

Regency Historical Romance

FOR THE LOVE OF AN EARL (Wicked Earls' Club)

A Humorous Aristocrat and Wallflower

Regency Romance Adventure

Earl of Wainthorpe — Book 1

Earl of Scarborough — Book 2

Earl of Keyworth — Book 3

Earl of Renshaw — Book 4

HEART OF A SCOT

A Passionate Enemies to Lovers

Scottish Highlander Historical Mystery

Romance Adventure

To Love a Highland Laird — Book 1

To Redeem a Highland Rogue — Book 2

To Seduce a Highland Scoundrel — Book 3

To Woo a Highland Warrior — Book 4

To Enchant a Highland Earl — Book 5

To Defy a Highland Duke — Book 6

To Marry a Highland Marauder — Book 7

To Bargain with a Highland Buccaneer — Book 8

A Christmas Kiss for the Highlander — Book 9

HIGHLAND HEATHER ROMANCING A SCOT: CASTLE BRIDES

A Passionate Enemies to Lovers Second Chance Scottish Highlander Mystery Romance

Heart of a Highlander — Prequel

The Viscount's Vow — Book 1

The Highlander's Heiress — Book 2

The Earl's Enticement — Book 3

Triumph and Treasure — Book 4

Virtue and Valor — Book 5

Heartbreak and Honor — Book 6

Scandal's Splendor — Book 7

Passion and Plunder — Book 8

SECRETS OF SCANDALOUS LADIES

A Romantic Class Difference Forced Proximity
Regency Romance with Aristocrats

THE CULPEPPER MISSES

A Humorous Wallflower Family Saga
Regency Romantic Comedy

The Earl and the Spinster — Book 1

The Marquis and the Vixen — Book 2

The Lord and the Wallflower — Book 3

The Buccaneer and the Bluestocking — Book 4

The Lieutenant and the Lady — Book 5

THE HONORABLE ROGUES®
A Second Chance Redeemable Rogue
and Wallflower Regency Romance

A Kiss for a Rogue — Book 1

A Bride for a Rogue — Book 2

A Rogue's Scandalous Wish — Book 3

To Capture a Rogue's Heart — Book 4

The Rogue and the Wallflower — Book 5

A Rose for a Rogue — Book 6

'Twas the Rogue Before Christmas — Book 7

A Rogue Worth the Risk — Book 8

ABOUT THE AUTHOR

COLLETTE CAMERON®

USA Today Bestselling author Collette Cameron® is renowned for her captivating, humorous, and heart-warming Scottish and Regency historical romance novels. With over 65 published titles, over 1.4 million books sold around the world, and multiple writing awards to her credit, Collette is a well-known author in the world of historical romance. Readers love her witty and relatable characters including daring rogues, dashing scoundrels, and the strong and spirited heroines who capture their hearts. From the rugged highlands to the refined drawing rooms of Regency England, Collette's novels will transport you to another time and place, where love and adventure are just a page away.

Collette's Sweet-to-Spicy Timeless Romances® are the perfect escape for readers looking for romantic escape, poignant inspiration, engaging humor, and entertaining stories.

Based in the Pacific Northwest, Collette is surrounded by the lush greenery and rainy skies that inspire her writing. She dreams of one day splitting her time between the Pacific Northwest and Scotland. In the meantime, she indulges in her love of all things cobalt blue, dachshunds, chocolate, and of course, crafting her next historical romance.

Blue Rose Romance® LLC
PO Box 167
Scappoose, Oregon 97056 USA
collettecameron.com

If you haven't joined Collette's exclusive mailing list scan the folloing QR Code to sign up!
You'll get access to exclusive content, sneak peeks,
contests, giveaways, and more...
(P.S. No spammy stuff.)

THE *Regency Rose*®

VIP CLUB

Follow Collette on social media.
Scan the following QR Code:

collettecameron.com

FOLLOW COLLETTE
ON
SOCIAL MEDIA